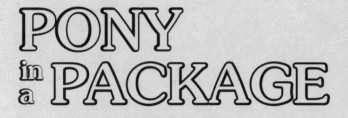

PONY in a PACKAGE

Previously published as *Pony in the Post*

Ben M. Baglio

Illustrations by Ann Baum

Cover illustration by
Mary Ann Lasher

AN
APPLE
PAPERBACK

SCHOLASTIC INC.

New York Toronto London Auckland Sydney
Mexico City New Delhi Hong Kong Buenos Aires

To Toyhorse Wonkytonks —
the smallest horse in Britain.

Special thanks to Linda Chapman.
Thanks also to C. J. Hall, B.Vet. Med., M.R.C.V.S., for reviewing
the veterinary information contained in this book and to Tikki Adorian
at the Toyhorse Stud, West Sussex, for all her help.

ISBN 0-439-34388-7

12 11 10 9 8 7 6 5   3 4 5 6/0

Printed in the U.S.A.   40
First Scholastic printing, December 2001

One

Mandy put some fresh bedding on the floor of the dog cage she had been cleaning out. "There you go, Honey," she said, turning to the golden retriever who was watching her from the cage opposite. "All ready for you again."

Every morning, Mandy Hope had the task of cleaning out the cages and feeding the animals that had stayed overnight in the residential unit at her parents' veterinary practice, Animal Ark. Before surgery began, Dr. Adam or Dr. Emily would check the animals over and give them any medication they needed. Today there was just Honey.

Mandy encouraged the dog to walk across into the now clean cage. Honey sniffed the bedding and slowly lay down, revealing a shaved stomach with a long row of neat stitches. "Good dog," Mandy murmured, crouching down to examine them. Two days ago, Dr. Emily had operated on the golden retriever to remove a large stomach tumor. The skin around the stitches looked pink and swollen and Mandy made a mental note to tell her mom.

Honey gently licked Mandy on the hand. Stroking the dog's silky ears, Mandy glanced at her watch and sighed. She would have loved to stay with Honey for longer but the first patients of the day would be arriving at nine and the clinic still needed to be set up. Saturday mornings were always busy at Animal Ark. "I'll be back later," she promised Honey, as she stood up and shut the cage door.

Dr. Emily was standing with her back to the sink in the kitchen, finishing a cup of coffee, when Mandy came in. "Morning, sweetheart," she said with a smile. The sun's rays filtered through the frosty window, picking up the lights in her long red hair. "How's Honey?"

Mandy explained about the swelling around the stitches.

Dr. Emily looked thoughtful. "It's probably just a simple allergic reaction," she said. Draining the last of her coffee she twisted her hair into a knot at the back of her head. "I'll go and check. Make sure you have some breakfast." As she left the room she called over her shoulder, "There are some Christmas cards that came this morning on the table."

Mandy shoved a piece of bread into the toaster and investigated the cards. *Only two weeks to go until Christmas,* she thought excitedly. *Only one more week of school!* Most of the cards were from owners of animals who came into Animal Ark. Mandy put them aside to take into the clinic later and went to the sink to wash her hands. She couldn't wait for Christmas!

Through the window she could see her dad scraping the ice off the windshield of his Land Rover. Simon, the veterinary nurse, was hurrying up the driveway, wrapped in a thick coat and scarf. The toast popped up. Mandy buttered and quickly ate it, tugged a hairbrush through her short, dark blond hair, and then went into the clinic, taking the Christmas cards with her.

In the Animal Ark waiting room, Jean Knox, the receptionist, was just turning on the computer. "Morning, dear!" she said cheerfully.

"Hi, Jean," Mandy said, adding the Christmas cards to the bulletin board. The clinic was looking very festive. Last weekend, she had decorated the walls with red and gold tinsel. She had even put up a tiny artificial Christmas tree behind Jean's desk.

Dr. Emily came in. "Honey's fine," she said to Mandy. "It's just as I thought. Nothing to worry about."

Mandy was relieved. "Oh, good." She got the mop and had just finished mopping the floor when the door opened and her father came in. "Has a package arrived for me?" he asked, stamping his feet on the mat.

"Dad! Shut the door!" Mandy exclaimed, as cold air flooded into the waiting room.

"We haven't had any deliveries yet," Jean said. "Are you expecting something special?"

Mandy grinned at her and squeezed out the mop in the bucket. "Dad ordered a new exercise machine. He's convinced that it's going to help him lose weight."

"It's a state-of-the-art machine," Dr. Adam said. "The catalogue assured me that this piece of equipment makes losing weight effortless and easy."

Dr. Emily looked up from examining the big red appointment book. "If you spend as much time using this exercise machine as you did looking through the catalogue and choosing it, you'll lose weight!" she said, chuckling.

"You both can laugh as much as you like," Dr. Adam said, looking at Mandy and Dr. Emily. "But just you wait, I'll be a new man by the new year."

Mandy hugged him. "Not too new," she said. "We love you just the way you are." She looked at his farm clothes. He had on a green flannel shirt, jacket, and sturdy brown shoes. "Where are you visiting this morning?" she asked.

"Beacon House first and then on to Greystones Farm."

Mandy was surprised. "Beacon House? Why are you going there?" Beacon House was a very modern house on a hill above the town. It was owned by the Parker-Smythe family and as far as she knew, the only animals there were seven-year-old Imogen Parker-Smythe's two rabbits — Button and Barney.

Dr. Adam looked surprised. "Didn't I tell you? The Parker-Smythes have bought Imogen a pony — an early Christmas present, I think — and they want me to check it over for them."

"A pony!" Mandy gasped, staring at him in amazement. "Imogen Parker-Smythe's been given a pony for Christmas and you forgot to tell me! Dad! How *could* you?"

Dr. Adam grinned at the expression on her face. "Sorry."

"So what's it like? How tall is it? How old? What color?" The questions tumbled out. Mandy could hardly imagine anything more exciting than getting a pony.

"Whoa!" exclaimed Dr. Adam, laughing and holding up his hands.

"What breed is it? What's its name?"

"Mandy! I don't know. I haven't seen it yet." Dr. Adam shook his head. "I'll tell you all about it when I get back."

"But Dad . . ."

"Bye," he said firmly and, turning, he escaped before Mandy could ask him anything else.

"Well!" she said, staring after him. "Imagine not telling me something like that!" She turned to find her mom shaking her head at her. "What?" Mandy demanded.

"Oh, Mandy," said Dr. Emily, smiling.

Just then, the door opened and in came the first couple of patients. Dr. Emily immediately whisked the first one into the examination room and Mandy hurried into the office to get a white coat. There was no time to stand around talking anymore. Morning clinic had begun!

As expected, Saturday morning clinic was very busy. Mandy hurried around getting things, answering the phone when Jean couldn't, soothing the pets who were waiting, and helping her mom and Simon in the exam rooms whenever she was needed. She loved having all the different animals to deal with. One minute it was a dog with a cut paw, then an aggressive rabbit, and then a cat who wouldn't eat its food. There was a constant stream of patients.

Halfway through the morning, Mandy came into the reception area and found a distressed-looking delivery-man standing at the desk. He was wearing a dark navy uniform and was holding a clipboard. "Well, where should I put it?" he was saying to Jean.

Jean was trying to talk to him and to a client on the phone at the same time. "Yes, yes, in a minute," she said to the deliveryman. "So, you want to make an appointment, Mr. Murray? When would be a good time?" she said into the phone.

"Listen, I'm in a bit of a rush," interrupted the man, his face breaking out into beads of perspiration. "Where do you want this crate to go?"

Jean covered the mouthpiece of the phone. "Oh, just put it in a corner somewhere," she said, waving her hand vaguely. "How about Tuesday afternoon, Mr. Murray?"

"But where?" the man persisted, looking around at the three dogs, two cats, and a rabbit who, with their owners, were filling the waiting room.

"Is this Dad's package?" Mandy asked, stepping forward. The man nodded. "You could leave it in the hall," Mandy suggested. "I'll show you where it is."

She was rewarded with a look of immense relief. "Thanks," the man said.

Mandy watched as he hurried to the van outside and unloaded an enormous wooden crate onto a trolley. He grabbed a brown package and clipboard from the van, shoved them on top of the crate, and brought everything into the hall. "Just sign there," he said to Mandy, fishing a pen out of his pocket and handing her the clipboard. He glanced at the box as she signed. "It's been very quiet," he said.

Mandy looked up in surprise. *Quiet? What did he mean?* But before she had a chance to ask, the man had grabbed the clipboard from her. "Great! Thanks!" He hurried out of the door with the trolley.

Mandy shrugged to herself and looked at the crate. It was made of wooden slats and had black bolts on one side. There was a white label on the side nearest to her with two red arrows pointing upward.

"Mandy! Can you come and help?" her mother called from the examination room. Mandy hastened back to work.

The crowd in the waiting room gradually lessened.

"Phew!" Mandy said to Jean, as the last patient went in to see Dr. Emily. "What a busy morning!"

"It's not over yet," commented Jean, seeing the door open again. But this time it wasn't another patient, it was Mandy's best friend, James, and his Labrador, Blackie.

"Hi!" James gasped as Blackie caught sight of Mandy and ran toward her. "Whoa, Blackie!"

"Hi!" laughed Mandy. "Hi, Blackie!" The dog bounced around her, his tail thwacking against her legs. Leaping up, he put both front paws on the counter, craned forward, and tried to lick Jean on the nose.

"Hello, Blackie," said Jean, hastily backing away from the long pink tongue.

"Blackie! Get down!" exclaimed James, pulling on the leash.

Mandy grinned at him. "Obedient as ever!"

"*Dis*obedient as ever!" sighed James. He managed to get Blackie under control, then pushed his glasses back up his nose.

Jean started to pick up a pile of papers that Blackie had knocked over with his paws. "Have you come for anything in particular, James?"

James shook his head. "Just to see Mandy."

Jean smiled and James immediately blushed. Mandy

glared at Jean. She and James were just good friends but he got embarrassed so easily. She hastily changed the subject.

"We've been really busy," she rattled on, as Jean turned back to the computer. "There's been loads of animals in. Johnny was in with Brandy and Mrs. Platt with Antonia." She broke off as she suddenly remembered the big news. "Oh, yes!" she exclaimed. "And you'll never guess what!"

"What?" said James.

"Imogen Parker-Smythe just got a pony!"

"Gosh," James said. "Isn't Imogen a little young?"

"She's seven," said Mandy. "She'll probably need a little help looking after it."

James smiled. "I can't imagine Mrs. Parker-Smythe helping to clean out a stable!"

An image of Imogen's mother flashed into Mandy's mind. She wore designer clothes, immaculate make-up, had perfect blond hair, and long pink fingernails. "Me, neither!" she grinned. "Dad's gone up to Beacon House to check it over. I can't wait for him to come back!"

Just at that moment, the door opened and Dr. Adam came in. "That's what I like to hear, a daughter's enthusiasm for her beloved father to return from a hard morning's work." His eyes twinkled. "This eagerness to see me couldn't have anything to do with a certain pony by any chance, could it?"

Mandy grinned. "It might." She hurried over. "What's it like?"

Dr. Adam thought for a minute. "Very nice," he said, and then, as if that was his last word on the subject, he took off his coat. "Hello there, Blackie," he said, bending down to pet the Labrador, who was sniffing around him.

"Dad!" Mandy exclaimed in exasperation. "I want to know *everything*!"

"All right," Dr. Adam said, his eyes twinkling. "Anything for a little peace. She's a palomino named Star with four white socks. She's thirteen hands high and perfectly healthy. She should be an ideal first pony." He started to look around the room. "She used to belong to Mrs. Parker-Smythe's twelve-year-old niece, who has apparently just moved into town with her mom."

Jean looked up from the computer. "Yes. They've moved into Willow Cottage on Walton Road. I saw the moving van there two days ago. I've been meaning to call and say hello."

Dr. Adam peered behind the desk.

Mandy stared. "What are you doing, Dad?"

He straightened up. "Hasn't my package been delivered yet?"

Mandy had forgotten all about the box that had been delivered earlier. "Yes. It's in the hall," she said.

"Great!" said Dr. Adam, rubbing his hands. "Effortless weight loss. Easy and enjoyable exercise." Mandy and James followed him through to the hall. Dr. Adam stopped and Mandy saw a look of surprise cross his face. "It's bigger than I expected!" he said, looking at the enormous wooden crate, half blocking the hallway.

Blackie pulled James over to the box and started frantically sniffing up and down the sides. "It looks like you open it at the front here," James said, pointing to the two black bolts. Blackie scratched the wood and whined. "Stop it, Blackie!" James exclaimed, pulling him away.

Dr. Adam frowned at the slatted sides of the box. "A box this big for exercise equipment? That seems a little strange." He walked forward to investigate his delivery. "If I didn't know better, I'd say these gaps between the slats were air vents."

Mandy laughed. "Since when has exercise equipment needed air vents, Dad?" As she spoke, the deliveryman's words flashed back to her: It's been very quiet, he had said. Her eyes widened. She dashed across to one of the air vents and peered in.

There in the darkness, something moved.

Mandy staggered back as if she had been shot.

"There's something in there!" she gasped, staring at her dad.

Dr. Adam hurried up beside her and peered in, too. Meanwhile, James looked at them as if he thought they'd gone crazy. "There's supposed to be," he said. "It's a package of exercise equipment."

Dr. Adam started to undo the bolts. "Well, whatever is in there, it's alive and definitely *not* exercise equipment! Stand back." He opened the door slightly and stared in. "Well, I never!" he breathed.

Mandy could hardly contain herself. "What is it, Dad?" she said, trying to peer around him.

Dr. Adam opened the door of the box.

There was a moment's pause, and then out trotted the tiniest black and white pony that Mandy had ever seen.

Two

The pony stopped and looked around the hall. It was wearing a bright red quilted stable blanket. Its head and neck were coal-black but its shoulders were white, splashed with distinctive black spots about the size of a quarter. It was no bigger than a large dog. Mandy, James, and Dr. Adam stared at it in stunned silence.

"It's a pony!" stuttered James at last. He struggled to hang on to Blackie, who was desperate to go and make friends with this new animal. "A pony in a package!"

"It's tiny!" gasped Mandy. She had never seen a pony so small. It looked at them curiously, large dark eyes peeping out from beneath an immensely thick, shaggy black forelock. *Who are you?* it seemed to say.

Mandy couldn't remember coming across anything so adorable in all her life. "Isn't it sweet!" she sighed, starting to walk cautiously toward it.

"Careful, Mandy, it might be scared," warned Dr. Adam. But the pony stepped forward to meet her in a friendly way.

Mandy took hold of its tiny red bridle. "There's a good pony," she soothed, stroking its neck. Its coat had been clipped and the hair felt rough against her hand.

Blackie pulled James over and the two animals sniffed noses. The pony was only a little bit bigger than the Labrador. Blackie jumped backward into a play bow, his front legs on the ground and his tail wagging hard. "He wants to play!" laughed James.

Mandy turned quickly to her father. "Where do you think it came from?"

"Who knows." Dr. Adam was investigating the wooden box. "But this *is* a decent traveling crate. It's got hay, water, and straw." He joined Mandy and James and, after letting the pony sniff at his hands, started expertly checking over its legs for any cuts and bumps. "Will you take off its blanket for me, please, Mandy?" he asked.

There were two straps around the chest and two that

crossed over underneath the pony's stomach to keep the blanket in place. Mandy quickly undid them and drew it back.

"Wow!" James exclaimed. The pony's back and hindquarters were a snowy white covered in large black spots, like the spots on a dalmatian.

Dr. Adam ran his hands over the pony's body, checked its teeth, and then put on the blanket again before the pony could get cold. "Well, he seems no worse the wear for his travels."

Mandy patted the pony's neck. "Why's he so small, Dad? Isn't he fully grown yet?"

"Oh, he's fully grown," said her father. "Four years old, I'd say, from looking at his teeth."

Mandy was astonished. "But he *can't* be fully grown. No pony's this small when it's fully grown."

Dr. Adam nodded. "Very true, but you see, this," he stood back, "is not a pony."

Mandy stared at him. Was her father kidding?

Dr. Adam smiled at her expression. "He's a spotted Miniature," he said as if that explained everything. "A Miniature horse."

"Isn't that the same thing as a pony?" James asked, looking confused.

Dr. Adam shook his head. "Miniature horses are bred to look more like very small horses than ponies. Do you see his fine legs and fine head? He's far more like a tiny Thoroughbred than a pony."

A Miniature horse! Mandy looked over the little animal. Yes, she could see it now. Apart from his size, there *was* something more horse-like than pony-like about him.

Dr. Adam patted the horse's neck. "When I was a student, one of the practices that I went to work at was with vets for a stud farm that bred Miniature horses. But I certainly haven't come across any of them in Welford." He rubbed his beard thoughtfully. "I've got a book about them somewhere."

"But why's he been delivered here?" Mandy demanded.

"There has to have been some mix-up," Dr. Adam said. "He must have been delivered to the wrong address." He started to examine the box for clues.

James helped. "Here's the address label!" he called out.

"What does it say?" Mandy asked.

"It's half ripped off," James replied. "It has part of an address and a name but it's not Animal Ark."

Dr. Adam looked over James's shoulder. "Miss Tania Bens —" he read out. "16 W —." He shook his head. "That's all that's left."

"Maybe the delivery man dropped your exercise

equipment at the house where the horse was supposed to go to and the horse here by mistake," Mandy suggested.

"Could be," said Dr. Adam.

"Tania Bens-something," said James thoughtfully. "I don't know anyone with that name in Welford."

Mandy looked at the horse and then at her dad. "What are we going to do with him, Dad?"

Dr. Adam scratched his head. "He should have come with a passport. It will have details of his pedigree and vaccinations and also his owner's address. Did the driver give you anything else, Mandy?"

Mandy remembered the brown package that had been delivered with the crate. "That package," she said.

But when Dr. Adam opened the package, he found that all it contained was a tiny green waterproof blanket. Nothing else. "Hmm," he said, looking at the horse. "So, there's no passport."

Suddenly, there was the sound of the hall door opening. "Let's see this exercise equipment . . . *oh my goodness!*" It was Dr. Emily coming in from the clinic. She stopped in the doorway and stared openmouthed at the little horse. Then she looked at Mandy and Adam. "This may be a silly question, but *what* is a Miniature horse doing in our hall?" she asked as the little horse walked forward to meet her.

Mandy explained. "So, you see, we think the delivery-man must have mixed up the packages," she finished.

Dr. Emily patted the horse and examined the torn label. "Well, I certainly haven't heard of a Tania Bens —. Maybe Jean or Simon will know."

Jean and Simon were called in and stood wracking their brains for someone in Welford with a name like the partial one on the label.

"It's a mystery," said Mandy. She grinned at her dad. "We'll just have to keep him."

"He *is* very sweet," said Jean.

"I think I'd better call the delivery company," Dr. Adam said hastily. "They should be able to sort this out."

As he hurried off, the little horse stamped his front hoof down on the hall carpet. "Maybe you should walk him around outside, Mandy," Dr. Emily suggested, opening the front door. Mandy encouraged the little horse out and led him up and down the Animal Ark driveway. James and Blackie walked alongside them.

"Isn't he beautiful?" Mandy said to James.

James nodded. "I still can't believe that he just arrived in a box, though!"

Seeing a clump of grass, the horse dragged Mandy toward it and thrust his head down. "He's stronger than he looks!" she said, laughing. She admired the horse's tiny pricked ears and the pretty black spots on his shoulders. Who did he belong to? She hoped it *was* someone in Welford. It would be so exciting to have a Miniature horse in town.

Dr. Adam opened the front door. "Well?" Mandy demanded, hurrying over.

Her father scratched his head. "The post office is closed for the weekend. I've left a message on their answering machine but they won't get that until Monday, now." He looked at the little horse with a frown on his face. "That leaves us with a problem — what do we do with him until then?"

"He'll have to stay here," said Mandy quickly.

"But, Mandy . . ." Dr. Emily began, coming out to join them.

Mandy had a feeling she knew what her mom was going to say. Her parents, particularly her mother, had very strict rules about not taking extra animals into Animal Ark. "We have enough responsibilities as it is to the sick animals who come in," her mother always said. But surely this was different.

"You've got to let him stay, Mom," Mandy pleaded. "After all, where else is he going to go?"

Dr. Emily looked undecided. "We could take him to the animal sanctuary. After all, we haven't really got the facilities to look after a horse."

"But he's not a stray," Mandy objected. "And the sanctuary is always so busy at this time of year. It's only for today and tomorrow. Don't you think he'll be fine in the yard since he's so small? I could clean out the shed so he's got some shelter."

Dr. Emily looked at Dr. Adam. He shrugged. "It *is* only till Monday and Mandy's right, Miniature horses don't need much space. The yard would certainly be big enough."

Dr. Emily gave in. "All right," she said, shaking her head as she looked at Mandy's delighted expression. "But you'll have to be responsible for him, Mandy."

"Oh, I will!" Mandy cried. "I'll look after him really well. And I'll borrow some hay and feed from Susan Collins." She spun around. "You'll help, won't you, James?"

James nodded eagerly. "There's a water bucket and hay net in the crate. We can use those."

Mandy flung her arms around the little horse's neck and hugged him. "You're going to be so happy here!" she told him.

The little horse nodded his head up and down. Mandy smiled. It was almost as though he understood.

Mandy and James led the horse into the long backyard at Animal Ark, and tied him to a sturdy tree. They swapped his red stable blanket for the waterproof New Zealand blanket that had come with him in the package. "This will keep you dry if it rains," Mandy said, as she kneeled down to fasten the buckles at the front. "And we'll make the shed nice and warm for you."

James went to get the rest of the things from the crate and Mandy started to clean up the yard. She blocked off the section where her three rabbits lived. "I'll clean your area out later this afternoon," she promised them, as she dragged some packing cases out from the shed to form a barrier. Flopsy, Mopsy, and Cottontail hopped happily around in their run, nibbling on the short winter grass.

James returned from getting the hay net and bucket from the crate, looking excited. "There's a name on the bucket!" he said, running across the yard and waving a black water bucket at Mandy.

Mandy read out the name painted in neat white letters around the side of the bucket. "Gabriel." She looked at the little spotted horse who was grazing on the grass under the tree. "Do you think that's his name?"

"There's one way to find out," said James.

"What's that?"

James took a step toward the horse. "Gabriel!" he called out loudly. The little horse pricked his ears and looked up. Yes, what? he seemed to say.

Mandy grinned. "Gabriel it is, then!"

It didn't take them long to clean up the yard and check that there were no poisonous plants that Gabriel might eat. They untied him and let him loose as they started to clean out the shed. Mandy carried an armful of tools around to the house and stopped to call her friend, Susan Collins, to see if they could borrow some hay, straw, and pony-nuts. Susan had a pony named Prince and was intrigued to hear about Gabriel. "He sounds gorgeous! I've always wanted to see a Miniature horse close up."

"Come over," Mandy offered.

"Okay, I'll get Dad to bring me over later with the hay and stuff. See you then!"

Mandy returned to the shed. Blackie seemed to think he was helping by grabbing buckets and plant pots and racing off at high speed around the yard with them. Gabriel watched him with a bemused expression on his face.

However, at last, even with Blackie's "help," the shed was empty, clean, and dust-free.

"All we need now is the straw, hay, and pony-nuts," said Mandy with a sigh of relief as she carried the last of the tools into the house and put them on some plastic in the study.

James followed her into the kitchen and collapsed into a chair. He ran a hand through his hair, making it stick up in all directions. "My arms ache!"

"Mine, too!" Mandy agreed, as she took down a couple of glasses from the cabinet. "Do you want some lemonade?"

As James nodded, the door opened and Dr. Adam popped his head in. "I thought I heard you come in," he said. "I found this and thought you might be interested in it." He handed a book to James. "See you later, I'm going out."

James read out the title of the book as the door shut behind Dr. Adam. "*The Miniature Horse* by L. M. Redmond."

Mandy put two glasses of lemonade and the cookie box on the table and sat down beside him. "What does it say?"

"Lots," said James, flipping through the pages. He stopped on a page that showed a picture of two Miniature horses pulling a cart and a picture of a child riding a Miniature horse. "Look, they can be ridden."

"By very small children," said Mandy.

James helped himself to a ginger cookie and turned to a chapter called "Care of the Miniature Horse." "It says here that Miniature horses can easily be kept on a

small plot of land providing they have regular exercise."
He looked up. "We'll have to take Gabriel for a walk tomorrow."

Mandy nodded. That sounded like a great idea. She
imagined walking through the town with Gabriel at
her side. People would really stare! She heard the
sound of a car outside and looked out through the
window. It was Susan and her dad. Draining the last of
her lemonade, Mandy went to open the front door. "Hi!"
she called to them. "Come and see him. He's in the
back."

Susan was enchanted with the little horse. "He's
tiny!" she said as he came over and nuzzled their hands.
She fed him a few pony-nuts, which he gobbled up in no
time, pushing against her pockets to see if there were
any more.

"He's in really good condition," Mandy said. "I just
wish we knew who he belonged to."

"I can't think of anyone named Tania in Welford," said
Susan. Gabriel pushed his head against her, demanding
attention. Susan smiled. "I'd like a Miniature horse. I'm
sure Prince would like the company."

"Oh, no," Mr. Collins said hastily. "One horse is *quite*
enough." He moved away from Gabriel. "Come on, I
think we'd better get that hay and straw unloaded from
the car."

Mandy and James helped carry the hay, straw, and pony-nuts to the yard. Susan had also brought them some old grooming brushes of Prince's. "It's really kind of you. Thanks," said Mandy.

"No problem," said Susan, getting into the car. "Why don't you walk him over to my house tomorrow? I'm sure Prince would love to meet him."

"That's a great idea!" said Mandy, looking at James, who nodded enthusiastically. "See you tomorrow!"

Mandy and James put down a bed of straw in the shed, filled the hay net, and gave Gabriel a couple of handfuls of pony-nuts in a bucket. Then James helped Mandy clean out Flopsy, Mopsy, and Cottontail's area.

As Mandy lifted the rabbits back into their hutches, James looked at his watch. "I'd better go. Mom will be wondering where I am." They arranged to meet at nine-thirty the next morning and then James biked home with Blackie trotting alongside.

Mandy woke up the next morning with a feeling that something exciting had happened. She lay in bed for a moment and then suddenly shot up as she remembered. Of course! *Gabriel!* She threw back her comforter and raced to the window. The little horse was grazing peacefully in the early morning light. His head was down, his blanket slightly askew.

After hurriedly dressing, Mandy ran down the stairs, opened the patio door, and went out.

"Gabriel!" she called softly.

The little horse looked up and then, with a gentle whinny of recognition, walked toward her. "Good morning," she murmured as he reached her. She stroked his neck. "Do you want some breakfast?"

It didn't take long to feed Gabriel and straighten his blanket. Then, leaving him to graze in peace, Mandy

hurried over to the residential wing to tend to Honey, the golden retriever.

James arrived after breakfast. They groomed Gabriel, cleaned out the shed, and then took him out for a walk toward Susan Collins's house on Walton Road. As they walked through the town, Blackie on one side of them, Gabriel on the other, they drew quite a lot of attention. Everyone they walked past wanted to stop and pet Gabriel and ask questions. The little horse seemed only too happy to be fussed over, nuzzling them and nibbling at their pockets. I like this place, his dark eyes seemed to say happily.

"I think Jean said that that's the house that Imogen Parker-Smythe's cousin has moved into," Mandy said, as she and James approached a small stone house with a sign outside saying Willow Cottage. It had a small square front yard and a path that led around to a yard in the back. There were some wooden packing crates and two chairs outside.

"It would be strange having Imogen Parker-Smythe as your cousin, wouldn't it?" said James as they walked Blackie and Gabriel past the house. "I mean, living in a normal house like this and having a cousin with a mansion with stables, a tennis court, and a helicopter pad."

"And a swimming pool," added Mandy. "Yes, very strange." Her eyes suddenly caught sight of a girl looking out of an upstairs window. She was staring at them. Mandy nudged James. "Look!" she said, smiling and raising her hand to wave at the girl. "That must be . . ." Her voice trailed off as the face withdrew abruptly and the curtains were pulled sharply across.

"Oh," Mandy said.

James frowned. "That was strange."

Mandy nodded. "Weird." She thought about it for a minute and then shrugged. "Oh, well, never mind. Maybe she didn't see us." She patted Gabriel's neck. "Come on, let's try a trot!"

With Blackie running alongside James, and Gabriel pulling at the lead rope, they charged up the road.

Three

After filling up Gabriel's evening water bucket and shaking out some more straw onto his bed in the shed, Mandy sat in a chair on the patio and watched him grazing his way slowly around the yard. She dug her hands deep into her pockets. It was cold but she wanted to make the most of every minute of having Gabriel there.

The little horse's teeth made a rhythmical tearing, chewing sound as he ripped up the grass. His ears twitched and his tiny hooves stamped into the lawn.

Whose horse are you? Mandy thought as she watched him work his way nearer and nearer to where she was sitting. "Good boy," she murmured as the little horse

31

reached the edge of the patio. Daintily, he stepped onto the patio and walked right up to her. She reached out to stroke him and he nuzzled at her hair. She giggled and ducked. "It's my hair, Gabriel! Not hay!"

"An easy mistake," Dr. Emily said, coming out of the house and onto the patio. She ruffled Mandy's untidy hair and patted Gabriel's neck. "He's adorable, isn't he?"

Mandy grinned. "And so friendly."

"Miniature horses normally are," said Dr. Emily. "They love people and they make great companions."

Gabriel wandered back onto the grass and for a while they both watched him. Then Mandy sighed and turned to her mother. "Where do you think he came from, Mom? And who do you think he belongs to?"

Dr. Emily put her hand gently around Mandy's shoulders. "I guess we'll find out tomorrow."

Mandy nodded and looked at Gabriel. Yes, Mom was right. Tomorrow they would find out.

The post office was still not open when Mandy left for school the next morning. "I'll call them later," Dr. Emily promised her. "And then we should be able to sort out this mix-up."

Mandy went around to the yard. "Bye, Gabe," she whispered, kissing his soft nose. He tickled her cheek with his lips and she felt her heart twist at the thought that he might not be there when she got home.

Dr. Emily opened the patio door. "Mandy! You'll be late."

With one last look at Gabriel, Mandy got on her bike and rode through the town to the Fox and Goose crossroads to meet James. He wasn't there. She stopped her bike by the curb and waited. Her mind was full of thoughts of Gabriel. Who was this Tania Benssomething who owned him and where did she live?

"Mandy!" A voice broke into her thoughts. A boy came hurrying toward her out of the Fox and Goose restaurant.

"John!" she said in surprise. "Hi! I didn't know you were home."

"Our last day was on Friday," John Hardy said. "Dad picked me up on Saturday. That's the good thing about boarding school. We have longer vacations!"

John went to a boarding school in the Lake District. Mandy had first become friendly with him a couple of vacations ago. "How are Button and Barney?" she asked. "Do you have them at the moment, or has Imogen?"

"I do. Dad and I got them yesterday." Button and Barney were two rabbits that John shared with Imogen Parker-Smythe. John looked after them during vacations whenever Imogen was away, and Imogen looked after them when John was at school. Mandy thought it was a very good deal because it meant that the two rabbits got lots of love and attention all the time.

"You'll have to come and see them," John told her, pushing a hand through his dark hair. "I'm keeping them *all* vacation." His eyes shone with pleasure. "Imogen's got a new pony and she's going to be busy with that for the next few weeks."

"Oh, yes!" In the excitement of having Gabriel around Mandy had virtually forgotten about Star, Imogen's new pony. "Have you seen the pony?"

"Just briefly," said John. He shrugged dismissively. "It was sort of gold-colored." He returned to a subject that interested him more. "You should see how much Button and Barney have grown. I'm going to make each of them a little stocking with rabbit treats for Christmas. You *must* come and see them."

"I will," promised Mandy. She saw James biking at great speed toward them and got back on her bike. "I'd better go or we'll be late for school. *Some* of us haven't gotten out yet. I'll call you when we do. Only another five days to go!"

James screeched up behind her as she started off. "Sorry, Mandy!" he gasped, pushing his glasses back up his nose. "I overslept!"

"What's new?" Mandy grinned. "Come on, I'll race you up the hill."

Once at school, Mandy and James went to their separate classes. "See you later!" Mandy called, slinging her bag onto her shoulder. Ms. Potter, her teacher, hated anyone being late.

But today it was Ms. Potter who was late. "You're lucky!" Susan Collins said, looking at the clock as Mandy thankfully sat down at the desk next to her. "How's Gabriel?" But before Mandy could answer, Ms. Potter came into the classroom. With her was a girl with blond hair whom Mandy didn't recognize. The girl glanced quickly around the class and then dropped her eyes to the floor.

There was a hasty shuffling of chairs and the sound of desk lids closing. "Good morning, class!" said Ms. Potter, putting her bag down on the desk and adjusting her large, round glasses.

"Good morning, Ms. Potter," the class replied. Mandy looked curiously at the girl. Who was she? Her shoulder-length hair fell like a curtain across her face.

Ms. Potter smiled at the class. "Well, everyone, I would like you to meet your new classmate, Tania Benster."

Mandy almost jumped out of her seat in surprise. *Tania Benster!* Just like the name on Gabriel's crate!

"Tania will be starting school with us after Christmas," continued Ms. Potter, "and so she is going to spend this week getting to know you all and getting to know the school." She pointed to an empty desk behind Mandy. "Go ahead and take that spare seat there, Tania."

Tania walked down the row of desks. The people she passed looked curiously at her but she stared at the floor, not meeting their eyes. Reaching the empty place she sat down.

Mandy swung eagerly around in her seat. "Do you . . . ?"

"No talking, please, Mandy," Ms. Potter interrupted, her voice firm. "Turn around. I want to take the attendance. You'll have plenty of time to get to know Tania later."

Mandy had to sit through attendance, almost bursting with excitement. She was longing to ask Tania about Gabriel. Was she his owner? Unable to resist a quick glance over her shoulder, Mandy saw that the new girl had taken a notebook out and was drawing on the cover. Mandy twisted around farther to see what she was drawing. It was a horse! At that moment, Tania looked up. Seeing Mandy watching her she quickly covered her drawing with her arm.

Mandy was about to whisper something when Susan nudged her. Ms. Potter had just read out Mandy's name for the second time. "Here, Ms. Potter!" Mandy said, swinging around hastily to face the front.

Ms. Potter finished taking attendance and gave out some notices. Then the bell rang and it was time for an assembly. The instant Ms. Potter told them to line up, Mandy seized her chance. "Hi!" she said excitedly to Tania. "I'm Mandy Hope. I live in Welford. Were you expecting a Miniature horse to arrive on Saturday?" Not waiting for Tania to answer, Mandy raced on. "Well, he was delivered to us instead! He had a label on his box that said 'Miss Tania Bens —' but we didn't know who that was so we kept him until we could get in touch with the post office. He's so sweet!"

Gradually, it began to filter through to her that Tania was just staring at her, not saying a word. "He *is* yours, isn't he?" Mandy asked.

Tania drew back. "No . . . no," she stammered, her face pale.

Mandy stared at her in surprise. "But he's got to be!"

"He's not!" Tania looked around the fast-emptying classroom as if she was trying to find a way to escape. "I . . . I don't know what you're talking about."

Mandy could hardly believe her ears. "But it said on the box, Tania Bens-something. Isn't that you?"

"No!" Tania exclaimed, jumping to her feet. "I told you, he's not mine! I hate horses! All of them. Now just leave me alone, okay?" Pushing past Mandy, she ran out of the classroom.

Mandy stared after her in astonishment.

"Well!" said Susan, who was standing beside Mandy. "What was all *that* about?"

"I don't know," Mandy said, as they hurried out of the classroom and down the hall. "I only asked if Gabriel was hers." She was taken aback by Tania's abruptness and felt very confused. "I was sure she was going to be Gabriel's owner," Mandy went on. "She's got the same name."

"Well, she's obviously not." Susan nodded her head up and down, causing her ponytail to bounce. "You heard what she said about hating horses. I'm certainly not going to be friends with *her* then!"

Mandy frowned. If Tania hated horses, then why had she been drawing one on the cover of her notebook? Surely if you hated horses, you didn't spend your time drawing them. "But . . ." she began.

"Shh!" said a teacher farther down the hall and Mandy quickly stopped talking.

Reaching the hall, she sat down on the floor with the rest of her class. She could see Tania sitting in the row in front. The new girl was staring straight ahead, hugging her knees tightly against her chest.

Mr. Wakeham, a teacher, stood up on the platform and started to speak, but Mandy hardly listened to a word. Tania's behavior in the classroom had just been so strange.

She glanced across at the new girl just in time to see Tania look up at the ceiling. For a fleeting moment, a look of despair crossed Tania's face. She looked so utterly desolate that Mandy caught her breath in shock. She didn't think she had ever seen anyone look so unhappy. Tania dropped her eyes to the floor. When she looked up, Mandy saw that the emotion was gone and her face was blank once more.

After the assembly, Mandy's class walked back to their classroom for English with Mr. Meldrum. Mandy was very quiet. She couldn't stop thinking of the look she had seen on Tania's face. *What could have happened to make her look so miserable?* she thought.

Susan Collins was still angry at the way Tania had spoken to Mandy. "I mean, who does she think she is?" she whispered to Mandy, as they walked down the hall. "You just don't go around blowing up at people like that."

"Maybe she's unhappy about starting a new school," Mandy said.

"Well, she still shouldn't have spoken to you like that," said Susan. "She's not going to make any friends that way."

"It can't be easy for her, Susan," Mandy protested, feeling a sudden urge to defend Tania. "Don't you remember what it was like when you started here?" Susan had moved from London to Welford and at first had found it hard to settle in. "You weren't exactly easy to get along with."

"I wasn't as bad as her!" Susan said indignantly. She stomped off to her desk.

Mandy was determined to try again with Tania. When she sat down she turned around in her chair. "I'm sorry if I upset you before," she said with an apologetic smile. "I didn't mean to."

Tania tucked a strand of blond hair behind her left ear and shrugged. "It's okay," she said. She looked away as if to end the conversation but Mandy wouldn't let her.

"Where was your last school?" she asked.

"York," Tania replied shortly.

"How long were you there?" Mandy asked.

"A long time."

"Was it good?"

"Yes."

Mandy struggled to keep the conversation going. "Why did you have to move?"

Tania's eyebrows drew together sharply. "Why do *you* have to ask so many questions?" she snapped.

Mandy was shocked by her directness. "Well . . . uh . . ."

"Look!" said Tania, glaring at her. "I just want to be left alone. Okay?"

Mandy turned around in her seat, her cheeks burning. Susan looked at her as if to say, "I told you so." And for once, Mandy was actually glad when Mr. Meldrum walked into the classroom and the lesson began.

At lunch, Mandy met James and told him all about the new girl. "First of all she gets mad at me because I ask her about Gabriel, and then she gets mad at me because I asked her why she moved," Mandy said, opening her bag of chips.

"She sounds strange," said James, as they walked over to sit on the wall.

Mandy nodded. "I think she's unhappy."

"I bet it can't be easy changing schools," James said. "I wouldn't like it."

Mandy was almost sure that there was more to Tania's unhappiness than just moving schools. She still had a clear memory of the despair on Tania's face during that moment in the assembly. What was it that was making her so miserable?

"Isn't it strange that she has the same name as the person Gabriel was supposed to have been delivered to?" James said. "It's a real coincidence."

Mandy nodded. James's words had made her think about Gabriel in the backyard at Animal Ark.

If Tania wasn't his owner, then who was?

Four

"Come on, James! I want to get home!" Mandy said, wheeling her bike quickly down the path. She was eager to get back to Animal Ark to discover if there was any news on Gabriel's owners.

As they reached the school gate they saw Tania getting into a beat-up-looking gray car. A woman with short blond hair was sitting in the driver's seat.

"Bye, Tania," Mandy called.

Tania didn't reply. She just got into the car and slammed the door. Since snapping at Mandy that morning she had hardly spoken to anyone all day.

"Friendly as ever!" muttered Susan Collins, who was walking past them and had witnessed the scene.

"Susan!" Mandy said, turning to her friend.

"What?" Susan demanded. "I don't know why you keep sticking up for her, Mandy."

"She's probably unhappy."

"Huh!" was Susan's reply.

"I wonder where Tania lives," Mandy said to James as they rode off.

James wasn't listening; he was standing up on his pedals and accelerating up the hill. "Race you when we get to the top!" he called over his shoulder.

Forgetting about Tania, Mandy accepted the challenge and charged after him.

A short while later, Mandy swerved up the Animal Ark driveway. Throwing her bike down outside the clinic, she hurried into the reception area. What was the news about Gabriel?

Dr. Adam was standing beside the reception desk, checking through the appointment book. "Hello," he said, looking up as she ran in. "Did you have a good day at school?"

But Mandy had only one thing on her mind. "Dad!" Her eyes searched his face. "What's happened about Gabriel? Have you found his owners? Is he still here?"

"He's still here," Dr. Adam replied, closing the appointment book. "But we *have* found his owners. The post office is supposed to be getting in touch with them."

"So who does he belong to?" Mandy demanded.

"A family named the Bensters. They've just moved into town. There was a mix-up with Gabriel and my exercise machine, like we thought. The deliveryman was in a rush because he had just heard that his wife had gone into the hospital to have a baby. He didn't read the addresses properly and just assumed that the horse would be going to the vet."

"So do the Bensters have your exercise machine?" Mandy asked.

Dr. Adam shook his head. "The deliveryman didn't have time to get to their house so he dropped it back at the depot. The company has promised to deliver it as soon as possible. They've also got Gabriel's passport there — something else the deliveryman forgot. They're going to send it to the Bensters."

"So Gabriel's still here for the moment?" Mandy said, happily.

Dr. Adam nodded. "At least until the Bensters get in touch."

"We had a new girl in school today named Tania Benster," Mandy told him, dumping her bag on a chair.

Dr. Adam looked surprised. "Gabriel's owner?"

Mandy shook her head. "She didn't know anything about him. It's really strange that she's got the same name though." She shrugged off her coat. "In fact, *she's* strange. She —"

Mandy broke off as the door opened and a woman with short blond hair came in. She was wearing a baggy sweater and jeans. Her face was worried. "Hello. I'm looking for Adam Hope," she said.

Dr. Adam stepped forward. "That's me. What can I do for you?"

The woman smiled. "My name's Sally Benster. I think you might have my daughter's Miniature horse here."

"Ah, Gabriel's mystery owner! Yes, we've got him," Dr. Adam said. "He's fine."

Mrs. Benster's whole face seemed to sag with relief. "Oh, that's such good news." She shook her head. "I can't tell you how worried I've been. Thank you so much for looking after him."

"No problem," said Dr. Adam. "Meet my daughter, Mandy. She's been doing all the hard work."

"My friend James helped me," Mandy put in. She smiled at the woman. "We've loved looking after him. He's wonderful."

Mrs. Benster looked at Mandy's school uniform. "You might have met my daughter. We've just moved here and she had her first day at school today. You're probably about the same age. She's twelve. She's named Tania."

"Tania!" Mandy exclaimed, feeling confused. "Yes, she was in my class." She shook her head. "But she *can't* be Gabriel's owner. She said she wasn't!"

"Oh." Mandy saw Mrs. Benster's face fall.

"Is there a problem?" Dr. Adam asked.

Mrs. Benster nodded. "Yes." She sighed. "Gabriel *is* Tania's horse. He was a present for her birthday on Saturday. But, well, she doesn't want him."

Mandy could hardly believe her ears. "Doesn't want him! Why not?"

Mrs. Benster ran a hand through her hair. "It's a long story," she said. "I'm sure you're both busy and don't want to hear my problems. Having Gabriel must have inconvenienced you enough already." She turned to Dr. Adam. "I'll arrange for him to be moved right away."

"There's no rush," Dr. Adam replied. "Look, why don't you come and have a cup of coffee? The clinic doesn't open tonight for another half hour. You can tell us the whole story. Maybe we can help."

"Well . . ." Mrs. Benster hesitated.

Mandy saw the indecision on her face. "I'll go make some," she said heading for the door. She was dying to know what was going on. "It's no trouble."

Mrs. Benster gave in. "Thank you," she said, smiling at her gratefully. "That would be very nice."

Once in the Animal Ark kitchen, Mrs. Benster started to explain the situation. "Tania's father and I got divorced recently," she said, stirring sugar into her mug of coffee. "I moved to Welford to be near my family. My sister and niece live here — the Parker-Smythes, do you know them?"

Dr. Adam and Mandy nodded. *So Mrs. Benster is Mrs. Parker-Smythe's sister,* Mandy thought. She wasn't what she had imagined at all!

"Tania chose to come and live with me," Mrs. Benster continued, "which has meant that she's had to cope with quite a few changes. We moved to a smaller house, got a smaller car, she had to change schools, and she had to sell her pony." She shook her head. "Tania loved Star so much. It's hit her really hard."

Mandy made the connection. "So Star is Imogen's new pony?"

Mrs. Benster nodded. "It seemed like such a good idea. Sonia, my sister, was looking for a pony for Imogen. I thought that Tania would still be able to see Star, maybe even ride her occasionally." She looked at her coffee. "But it hasn't worked out like that. At the moment, Tania's refusing to go anywhere near Star. She won't go and see her and she won't visit her father either. She just seems so unhappy."

"So how does Gabriel fit into the picture?" Dr. Adam asked curiously.

Sally Benster took a long sip of her drink. "Well, Gabriel was Sonia's idea," she explained. "She had seen an article on Miniature horses in a magazine and thought that if Tania had a Miniature horse it would help make up for losing Star. It seemed an ideal solution. The yard at our new house is large enough for a Miniature horse and they're not too expensive to feed. I agreed and so Sonia bought Gabriel. He was going to be a surprise birthday present for Tania on Saturday. Anyway, then he didn't arrive and so I had to tell Tania about him and . . . well . . ." Her voice trailed off.

"She didn't react well?" Dr. Adam asked quietly.

"It was awful," said Mrs. Benster, shaking her head and looking upset. "She just exploded, said that she hated horses and that she never wanted one again. She even threatened to run away if I brought Gabriel to the house." She shook her head. "I don't know what to do."

Tania's strange behavior that day at school was suddenly starting to make sense to Mandy. She tried to imagine what it must be like to lose so many things at once: your home, your father, your friends, and your pony. *Poor Tania — and poor Gabe,* she thought. "What will happen to Gabriel?" she asked Mrs. Benster.

"Sonia has offered to let him stay in Star's stable up at Beacon House for the moment," Mrs. Benster replied. "We're just going to see what happens. If Tania still feels the same way after Christmas then I suppose I'll just have to sell him."

Mandy felt her heart sink. She didn't want Gabriel to move away having only just met him.

"I'm sure Tania'll come around," Dr. Adam said.

"I hope you're right," sighed Mrs. Benster. "But she can be so stubborn at times." She put down her mug. "Thank you. To tell you the truth it's been a relief to talk about all this. You've been very kind." She stood up. "I'll arrange to have Gabriel moved as soon as possible."

Dr. Adam got to his feet. "No need to do that. We can drop him off at Beacon House for you. His crate should fit into the Land Rover." He walked to the back door. "Now, why don't you come and meet him."

Mrs. Benster followed Mandy and Dr. Adam into the backyard. "Oh, he's tiny!" she cried as she saw Gabriel grazing happily, wearing his New Zealand blanket. She went over to pet him. "Isn't he adorable?"

Yes, thought Mandy as the little spotted horse looked up at them with pricked ears, *he is.* But the challenge was to make Tania realize that, too.

*   *   *

The following morning, just as it was getting light, Dr. Adam stopped the Land Rover outside Beacon House. "I'll go and let Mrs. Parker-Smythe know we're here." He jumped out and crunched across the gravel to the grand front door.

Mandy looked at the large white house. It was flanked on one side by a tennis court, on the other by a helicopter pad. "Imagine living in a house like this," she said to James. "Just think how many animals you could have!"

James yawned and nodded halfheartedly. Mandy grinned. James hated getting up early but he had been determined to come with them to drop Gabriel off.

Dr. Adam hurried back. "We're going to drive Gabriel around to the stables and unload him there," he said.

The gardens at the back of Beacon House were beautifully landscaped with a pond and an orchard and rows and rows of carefully tended flower beds. The stables were a little to one side behind high hedges. "I never even knew there were stables here," Mandy said to her dad as he drove down a small driveway and stopped outside a redbrick block of three stables and a tack room. Behind the stables was a paddock.

"That must be Star!" Mandy exclaimed, seeing a pretty palomino pony grazing. Almost before Dr. Adam had stopped the Land Rover, Mandy was leaping out. She raced over to the paddock. James followed her.

"Isn't she beautiful?" Mandy breathed as they leaned over the five-bar gate and looked at the pony. Star lifted her head, noticing them from a distance. Her coat was the color of pale gold and her mane and tail were cream. On her forehead was a diamond-shaped splash.

"That's Star," said a high-pitched voice behind them. They turned and saw a mousy-haired, slightly over-weight girl coming toward them. "She's my new pony."

"Hi, Imogen," Mandy with a smile. When she had first met Imogen, the little girl had been spoiled and rude but ever since she had been given the rabbits — Button and Barney — she had become far less selfish and more friendly and outgoing.

Imogen reached into the pocket of her bright red jacket and took out a carrot. "Star!" she called. "Come and say hello." Star walked over to the gate but stopped just out of reach. Imogen held out the carrot temptingly. "Come on!" The palomino pony came forward but as soon as Imogen tried to take hold of her bridle she jumped back and trotted away.

Mandy saw Imogen's face fall. "Does she do that of-ten?" she asked the little girl.

Imogen nodded. "It took two of the gardeners half an hour to catch her yesterday." Mandy saw her lower lip

quiver slightly. "I don't think she likes me." Imogen
stared at her pony, who was now grazing again.

"Oh, I'm sure she does," Mandy said quickly.

"Ponies are often difficult to catch," James added. "It
doesn't mean they don't like you."

"Really?" said Imogen, looking hopeful.

Just then, Dr. Adam called to them. "Mandy! James!
Can you give me a hand getting Gabriel out, please?" He
had opened the back of the Land Rover. Beside him
stood a lady who was looking uncertainly at the large

crate. She was wearing a very new-looking green jacket, a yellow silk scarf, leather gloves, and a pair of light beige trousers that had been tucked into the cleanest green boots that Mandy had ever seen.

"Hello, Mrs. Parker-Smythe," Mandy said, reaching the Land Rover.

Mrs. Parker-Smythe smiled. "Good morning, Mandy." Even though it was early in the morning, Mandy noticed that she was already perfectly made up. "Has Immi been showing you her new pony?"

Mandy nodded.

Dr. Adam attached a ramp to the back of the Land Rover and opened Gabriel's crate. Gabriel looked out and surveyed the scene. What have we here? he seemed to say.

"It's all right, Gabe," Mandy murmured, taking him by the halter. "This is where you're going to live for a while." She led him down the ramp and let him have a good look around.

Imogen fed him carrots from her pocket, laughing as his lips tickled her hand. "He's cute!"

"He looks even smaller here than he did at his breeders," Mrs. Parker-Smythe said, patting him gingerly.

"I wonder how he'll get along with Star," James said.

"There's only one way to find out," Dr. Adam replied.

Mandy led Gabriel to the paddock. Seeing Star, his ears pricked up and he quickened his pace. Star walked curiously toward the gate. "Should I just let him go, Dad?" Mandy asked.

Dr. Adam nodded as he unlatched the gate. "They should be fine."

Mandy unclipped the lead rope and Gabriel trotted eagerly into the field toward Star. He stopped a short distance away. Star and Gabriel extended their heads until their muzzles were almost touching. There was a long pause while they blew down their nostrils at each other. Mandy crossed her fingers. She had seen ponies do this before and knew that sometimes they would squeal and strike out at each other, but this time it didn't happen. Star and Gabriel dropped their heads and started to graze contentedly side by side.

"They're friends!" said Imogen, and everyone smiled.

Dr. Adam turned to Mrs. Parker-Smythe. "Will you be all right looking after them both?"

"I hope so," Mrs. Parker-Smythe replied, a slight frown creasing her face. "Sally assured me that Gabriel shouldn't be too much trouble, but you see, Imogen's father and I don't really know that much about horses. We've got a part-time groomer starting after Christmas. I thought we'd be all right until then because Tania was

supposed to have been helping out, but . . . well . . ."
She cast a quick look at Imogen. "That hasn't worked
out."

"Tania's too busy moving right now," Imogen an-
nounced. "That's why she can't have Gabriel and why
she can't help, isn't it, Mommy?"

"That's right, darling," Mrs. Parker-Smythe said.

Mandy and James exchanged glances. Obviously
Imogen had not been told the real story.

Mrs. Parker-Smythe looked at the ponies and sighed.
"I suppose Immi and I will just have to manage as best
we can until the groomer starts."

Mandy suddenly had an idea. "We could help," she offered eagerly. "Couldn't we, James? We get off from
school on Friday."

"We'd love to," James said.

"Oh, yes, Mommy! Yes!" said Imogen. "It would be
fun!"

Mandy looked hopefully at Mrs. Parker-Smythe. "Are
you sure?" Mrs. Parker-Smythe said to her.

"Definitely!"

Mrs. Parker-Smythe turned to Dr. Adam. "Would that
be all right with you?"

"Certainly," said Dr. Adam. "It seems an ideal solution. Good for the horses, and good for you."

"And great for us!" said Mandy, grinning at James. Now, they wouldn't have to say good-bye to Gabriel after all. They could come and see him every day.

Gabriel wandered near the gate. Imogen ducked underneath the fence and took a handful of carrots over to him.

Mrs. Parker-Smythe shook her head as she watched Gabriel gently take the carrots from Imogen's outstretched palm. "Sometimes I wonder if I've done the right thing," she said quietly so Imogen wouldn't hear. "Buying Gabriel seemed like such a good idea at the time. I thought Tania would be delighted. The woman at the breeders told me that Miniature horses have a nickname — they are called the Ambassadors of Goodwill. I suppose I hoped that Gabriel could be an Ambassador of Goodwill for Tania, helping her get used to the changes in her life, but, well," she shook her head, "I'm beginning to wonder whether I've done more harm than good." She sighed and then seemed to pull herself together. "Can I offer you a cup of coffee, Dr. Adam?" she said.

Dr. Adam shook his head. "We'd better get going or Mandy and James will be late for school." He started walking toward the Land Rover with James. "Come on, Mandy," he called over his shoulder.

Mandy was looking at Gabriel. Tania just *had* to accept him.

"Mandy!" her father called.

"Coming!" Mandy called. She looked again at the little horse. "I'll persuade her, Gabe," she whispered. "Just you wait and see."

Five

When she got to school, Mandy hurried to her class's cloakroom. She stopped in the doorway. Tania was taking off her coat, her back to the door. Mandy was suddenly aware of how awkward a meeting this could be. What did she say? Did she admit to knowing that Gabriel was Tania's or did she pretend she didn't know anything?

Tania turned and froze, a look of confusion and embarrassment crossing her face as she saw Mandy standing there.

Mandy made a quick decision. It was better to be

up front. "Hi," she said, going forward with a friendly smile. "I met your mom last night and she told me that Gabriel was yours. She told me about you not wanting him," she hesitated, "and about the divorce."

Tania flinched, two bright red spots of color springing into her cheeks.

Mandy hurried on. "My dad and I took him up to your aunt's this morning. We put him in Star's field. She seems to like him."

"I don't care," Tania said in a low, determined voice. She went to walk past Mandy. "I told Mom to get rid of him."

"But why?" Mandy said, stopping her. "He's great."

"He's a Miniature horse!" Tania exclaimed, shaking her arm free from Mandy. "What good are they?"

"Lots!" Mandy said. "They pull carts, you can train them to be driven, and there are shows for them. They can even be ridden by small children." She had been reading her father's book.

"Exactly!" Tania said angrily. "They're for babies! They're not real horses. They're just for people who can't afford real horses."

"That's not true!" Mandy said. "Look, just come and see him. You'll love him."

Tania shook her head. "No way! Mom should never have taken him to Aunt Sonia's. I told her I didn't want him. Well, I'm not going to change my mind." She pushed past Mandy.

"But he'd make you so happy!" Mandy exclaimed after her.

Tania swung around. "Happy?" There was a pause during which she looked at Mandy in utter disbelief and then she shook her head. "How can I ever be happy again?" She ran out of the cloakroom, but not before Mandy had seen tears welling up in her eyes.

At lunch, Mandy talked things over with James. "I know it's just because she's angry and upset about the divorce and everything," she sighed as they sat on the wall outside. "But if she actually came to see Gabriel, I'm sure she'd want to keep him. The trouble is how do we *get* her to meet him? She refused to come and see him."

James looked thoughtful. "It's almost vacation. Maybe we could take Gabriel for walks down to her house and hope to bump into her."

"Of course!" Mandy exclaimed. "If Tania won't come to see Gabe then we'll take him to see her! That's a fantastic idea, James!"

"We could take him on Saturday," said James. "And then again on Sunday."

"And then on Monday," Mandy said. "If she sees him often enough she's bound to fall in love with him!" She grinned. "It's a great plan! We'll have changed her mind by Christmas, you'll see!"

But when she told her mom that evening, Dr. Emily looked doubtful. "Remember, Tania's been through a very difficult time, Mandy," she warned, as she put a young rabbit with a freshly bandaged leg back into a cage. "It may take some time before she's ready to come to terms with her new life."

Mandy helped clean up the old dressing. "But if she keeps seeing Gabriel I bet she won't be able to resist him."

Dr. Emily tucked a strand of hair behind her ear. "It's worth a try, but don't be disappointed if it doesn't work, sweetheart. I think it sounds like Tania needs some time and space at the moment."

Mandy understood what her mom was saying but it didn't matter. She still felt convinced that the plan would work.

Dr. Emily opened the door of Honey's cage. The golden retriever was looking far more cheerful than she had a few days ago.

"She's much better," Mandy said, as Honey came out, wagging her tail.

Dr. Emily nodded. "I called her owners. They're coming to get her tomorrow." She opened the cage door and bent down to inspect Honey's stitches. "Healing up nicely," she said.

"I'll miss you," Mandy said, kneeling down and stroking Honey's face. "But at least you'll be home for Christmas." Honey wagged her tail. Mandy smiled. It was always hard saying good-bye to animals, but there was nothing better than seeing an animal being reunited with its happy owners. Mandy gently scratched Honey's silky ears. As much as she would miss her, she knew that Honey would be glad to go home.

The next morning, before school, Mandy biked up to Beacon House to check on Gabriel and Star. She tapped the security code that Mrs. Parker-Smythe had given her the day before into the black box by the entrance. The electric gates swung open smoothly. Mandy biked up the long driveway and around to the stables.

"Hi!" Imogen came running to meet her. "Will you help me catch Star?"

They walked down to the paddock and called the ponies. Gabriel walked eagerly toward them but Star tossed her head and walked away. "She did this yesterday," Imogen told Mandy. "I couldn't catch her at all and there was no one to help. Daddy was at work and Mommy had friends for lunch and it was the gardeners' day off."

"Don't worry, we'll get her," Mandy said. She looked at Star, who had stopped a little way down the field. "If we take Gabriel in and then bring out a bucket with some pony-nuts in it, she might come."

Imogen nodded. "Okay. But I bet it will take forever." She opened the gate for Mandy to lead Gabriel through.

"Come on, Gabe," Mandy said, clicking her tongue.

Gabriel looked over at Star and whinnied gently.

"Look!" said Imogen suddenly.

Star had started walking toward them; she was looking at Gabriel. Imogen held out a carrot and Star walked all the way over. The pony stopped and glanced at Gabriel, who gave another reassuring whinny and then Star took the carrot daintily from her hand.

"Good girl!" Imogen cried, clipping on the lead rope. She turned to Mandy, her eyes shining with excitement. "She's never done that before!"

Mandy grinned. "It must be Gabe. He's a good influence!"

They took the two animals to the stables and fed them their breakfasts. Then Mandy showed Imogen how to check them over for any cuts or lumps.

"I know how to groom," Imogen said, taking a dandy brush out of her grooming kit. "We learned at my riding school."

The two girls settled down to grooming the ponies.

Imogen soon had a smudge on her nose and dust in her hair. Mandy smiled. It was amazing how animals brought out the best in people, she thought, as she watched Imogen kiss Star's nose.

"Mommy says I can't ride her till the weekend when you and James are here," Imogen said. "But I'm going to groom her a lot." She smiled happily and picked up a soft body brush to use on Star's face. "Star's won lots of prizes. Tania used to have all her prizes on a wall in her bedroom. Mommy says that when Tania's not as busy she's going to come and teach me. I can't wait."

Imogen chattered on until it was time for Mandy to change into her school clothes and bike back down the hill. "See you tomorrow," she called to Imogen as she got on her bike. Imogen was still grooming Star. She waved happily and Mandy rode away.

For the rest of the week, Tania ignored Mandy at school. She hardly spoke to anyone and sat by herself at lunchtime, seeming to retreat more and more into her own unhappy thoughts. Mandy became more and more convinced that Tania needed Gabriel. Surely, she wouldn't be able to stay so miserable if she had a horse to think about and love.

It was raining a little when Mandy got up on Saturday morning but she didn't care. It was the first day of vacation and she leaped out of bed with a broad grin on her face.

"You look happy!" Dr. Emily said, as Mandy raced down the stairs.

"That's because I am!" Mandy exclaimed. "Two weeks without school and it's almost Christmas! Only one more week to go. I can't wait!"

Dr. Emily laughed. "Do you want a ride up to Beacon House later?"

"Yes, please!" Mandy said eagerly. "I'll call James and tell him to come over." She helped herself to an orange. Today was the first day of their plan to get Tania to accept Gabriel. She was determined that it was going to work!

When Dr. Emily dropped Mandy and James at Beacon House after morning clinic, Imogen came running out to meet them. "Hooray!" she said. "I can ride Star now!"

James looked at Mandy. "We'll walk Gabe later," she said. She could see from Imogen's face that the little girl was about to burst with excitement.

Star shook her head and stamped her feet as they tacked her up and Imogen mounted. "She looks lively," James whispered to Mandy as Imogen set off around the paddock.

"Are you all right?" Mandy called to Imogen. Star was pulling and tossing her head.

"Fine!" Imogen called back but Mandy could hear a shake in her voice. Then Star shied and Imogen shortened her reins, making Star pull even more. Imogen leaned forward rather nervously. Star sidestepped and jogged. "She doesn't look fine," Mandy said.

"What should we do?" James said.

Mandy had a sudden idea. "I'll be back in a minute," she said, running for the stables. She returned a few minutes later leading Gabriel.

"What are you doing?" Imogen called.

"He was lonely," Mandy lied. Gabriel looked at Star for a few moments and then put his head down to graze. Just as Mandy had hoped, having Gabriel nearby seemed to relax the palomino pony. She stopped jogging as much and Imogen loosened the reins.

Mandy hugged Gabe. The effect he had on Star was wonderful. Mandy crossed her fingers. She hoped he would have the same effect on Tania, too!

After brushing Star down, Imogen went Christmas shopping with her mom and dad and Mandy and James were at last free to take Gabriel down to town.

It was quiet on the road. Only the soft clip-clopping of

Gabe's unshod hooves and the occasional cry of a bird circling overhead broke the stillness of the air.

James frowned. "What if Tania isn't in?"

"We keep coming back until she is," Mandy replied. She was determined their plan was going to work.

They approached Willow Cottage. "What should we do when we get there?" James asked, pushing his hair back from his forehead. "Just walk him back and forth outside?"

Mandy nodded. She hadn't really thought beyond the initial plan of taking him to Tania's house. A thought struck her. *What if Tania just stayed inside and refused to come out and see Gabriel?* Knowing Tania, it seemed quite likely. Mandy pushed the thought away. *Think positive*, she told herself firmly.

"It doesn't look like there's anyone in," James said as they reached the house. There were no lights on inside.

"Tania might be there," Mandy said. "Come on, let's walk him around." They led Gabriel up and down the road several times. But there wasn't any sign of movement from the house. At last, even Mandy had to admit that they were wasting their time.

"So what do we do now?" James asked, stopping.

"Come back later," Mandy said, trying to sound positive.

James raised his eyebrows slightly. "So we walk all

the way back to Beacon House and then turn around and come back?"

"Yes," Mandy replied, beginning to realize the second problem with their plan. It was all well and good to say they would keep coming back until Tania was in, but it was actually a far walk from Beacon House down to Willow Cottage. She had an idea. "We could take him to visit Susan and then come and see if Tania is in on our way back."

Susan lived outside the town, farther down Walton Road. James shrugged. "Okay. It's better than walking all the way back up the hill right now, I suppose."

They set off down the road. "There's Prince!" said Mandy, pointing. The bay gelding was grazing in a field just to the side of The Beeches, Susan's large house. A figure was standing beside the stone wall watching him.

"Isn't that Tania?" James said.

Mandy nodded. "This is perfect! Now she's going to have to see Gabe!"

As they got closer, Tania heard them. She started to walk swiftly away in the opposite direction.

"Tania!" Mandy called. "Wait!"

Tania stopped and turned slowly around.

Gabriel, eager to say hello to this new person, dragged Mandy forward until he reached Tania. Hello, he seemed to say, nudging her with his nose. Who are you?

Have you got any treats? For a fleeting second, a smile lit up Tania's face as she looked down at him and automatically she reached out to stroke his neck.

"He's beautiful, isn't he?" Mandy said eagerly.

Tania pulled her hand away and stepped back. Gabriel followed her. She pushed him away. Gabriel pushed back. A new game! he seemed to think. He pulled determinedly toward Tania with Mandy hanging on at the end of the lead rope. No matter how far Tania retreated, he followed her. Despite herself, Tania's lips

started to twitch. "Go away!" she half laughed, pushing him again. "Go on!"

Gabe refused to listen. Mandy was delighted. "He likes you," she said to Tania. "Look at the way he is trying to get to you."

The smile instantly vanished from the other girl's face. "I don't want him to like me!" she said.

Mandy looked at her in astonishment. "Why not?"

Tania's eyes looked almost desperate. "I just don't! Okay?"

"But, Tania . . ."

Tania turned and ran down the road.

James looked at Mandy in confusion. "What did she mean by that?"

"I don't know," said Mandy, equally mystified. She frowned, watching her disappear. What possible reason could Tania have for not wanting Gabriel to like her? It just didn't make any sense. She patted the Miniature horse's neck. "Well, *we* like you, anyway," she told him.

"So what are we going to do now?" James asked.

"Try again tomorrow," Mandy said. Determination flooded through her. "Whatever she says, we're not going to give up!"

Six

"Mommy says I can take Star down the road today if you come with me," Imogen said as she ran to meet Mandy and James the next morning.

Star tossed her head as they tacked her up. She stamped her foot and sidestepped as Mandy tried to tighten up the girth. It was windy and the wind seemed to be making her livelier than ever.

"Steady, girl," said James, who was holding on to her bridle.

Mandy tried again, but Star danced around. "I'll put it on the last few holes just before you get on," she said to Imogen, who was putting on her hard hat. Star tossed

72

her head high. Mandy frowned. "Are you sure this is a good idea, Imogen? It might be better to wait until a less windy day before you take her out."

"No, I want to go today," Imogen said, with just a hint of the spoiled child she had once been creeping into her voice. "Mommy said I could."

Mandy reluctantly gave in. If Mrs. Parker-Smythe had said it was okay then she couldn't really argue.

"Maybe we should get Gabe," James said to her in a low voice. "It might keep Star a little calmer."

"Good idea," Mandy said, taking the reins from him.

"I want to get on!" said Imogen.

"Let me tighten her girth first," Mandy said, as James went to the paddock to catch Gabriel. She lifted the saddle flap, trying to hold on to the reins at the same time. There was a gust of wind. Star suddenly whipped around, Mandy lost hold of the reins, and the next instant Star was running off down the driveway.

"Star!" cried Imogen in a panic.

"Oh, no!" gasped Mandy.

"Quick!" said James. Mandy and James dashed after the fast-disappearing pony.

"It'll be okay!" James said, as they charged down the driveway. "The gates will be shut at the end. They always are. We'll catch her there."

"When we get near her don't run!" said Mandy.

They raced around the bend in the driveway expecting to see Star waiting by the gates. But the gates were wide open. Star was nowhere to be seen.

"Come on!" James exclaimed to Mandy. "We've got to stop her!" They started running down the hill.

Mandy's heart pounded. Although the winding, narrow road that led down from Beacon House to the town was quiet, the road at the bottom of the hill could be very busy. If Star got onto it, there was no knowing what could happen. Mandy knew she would never forgive herself if anything happened to Star. *Oh, why didn't I keep hold of the reins?* she thought.

"There!" gasped James as they ran around a bend in the road. They both stopped dead. Star was grazing in a gateway, just ahead.

Mandy's heart leaped. "Star!" she called. She rustled a candy paper in her pocket and the pony looked up. Mandy knew that they had to keep as calm as possible. What they didn't want was Star to get frightened and run off again. "There's a good girl!" Mandy said in as soothing a voice as she could. She walked slowly forward, rustling the candy paper again and holding out her hand. "Come here. Good girl."

Pricking her ears curiously, Star took a step toward her but then, just at the wrong moment, Imogen came running around the bend. "Star!" she cried out in delight. The pony started in alarm and, wheeling around, trotted off down the road, the reins flapping dangerously near her legs.

"Imogen!" Mandy exclaimed in dismay.

A figure came walking around a bend in the road ahead.

"It's Tania!" cried James.

Tania saw Star trotting toward her and leaped into the pony's path. "Star!" she cried. The pony stopped dead and snorted wildly. Tania held out a hand. "Here, girl," she said softly.

Grabbing onto Imogen in case she made any sudden move, Mandy and James watched as Star lowered her head and walked straight over to Tania and pushed affectionately at her with her head. Tania gently touched Star's face.

Imogen pulled free from Mandy and James and raced down the road. "Tania! Tania!" she cried, her voice high and excited. "You caught her! Thank you! Thank you so much!"

Star leaped back and Tania grabbed her reins only just in time. "Stop it!" she called out to Imogen. "Stop running!"

The little girl stopped. The shock on Tania's face turned to anger. She marched toward Imogen. "Don't you understand, Imogen?" she demanded, her eyes blazing. "What do you think you are doing, running toward a pony who's excited?" She didn't give Imogen a chance to speak. "And what's Star doing loose on the road anyway?"

"She escaped," Imogen stammered, taken aback by Tania's anger. "I was about to get on."

"She could have ended up in an accident!" Tania exclaimed.

"I know. I'm sorry," Imogen whispered, her face starting to crumple.

"Sorry isn't good enough!" Tania's voice was shaking with emotion. "What good is it to be sorry when Star's lying dead at the end of the road? You don't deserve to have a pony, Imogen!"

Mandy hurried over. "Tania!" she exclaimed. "It's not Imogen's fault." Tania glared at her. "It's not," Mandy insisted. "*I* was holding Star when she escaped. If anyone's to blame, it's me, not Imogen."

Tania paused. She glanced at Star and suddenly the anger seemed to drain from her face. She thrust the reins at Mandy. "Here," she said. "Take her." Before Mandy could say anything she had turned and walked off down the road.

"Tania!" Imogen called after her, the tears rolling down her cheeks.

Mandy hesitated. Should she go after Tania? Or should she stay and comfort Imogen?

James seemed to read her thoughts. "Go on," he said quietly, reaching for Star's reins. "I'll look after Imogen." He put an arm around Imogen's shoulders. "Come on, Immi. Let's take Star back."

Mandy ran after Tania. She had stopped a little way down the road and was staring down the hill, her back to Mandy.

Mandy slowed as she reached her. *This could be difficult*, she thought. "Are you all right?" she asked.

Tania nodded and sniffed but didn't turn around.

"I know Imogen shouldn't have run up like that, Tania," Mandy said. "But it wasn't her fault that Star escaped." There was a pause and then she saw Tania give a faint nod. "Star's really too much for her," said Mandy, feeling encouraged. "Couldn't you come and help?"

There was no reply.

"Tania?"

Tania swung around. Her pale cheeks were damp with tears. "You don't get it, do you?" she cried intensely, a catch in her voice. "Star should be *mine*, not Imogen's. Every time I see her it reminds me of —" She broke off, shaking her head. "It just reminds me," she said more quietly.

"But you've got Gabriel now," Mandy said.

"Gabriel?" said Tania. "A useless Miniature horse!"

Anger rose in Mandy. "He's not useless!" she exclaimed. "He's friendly and affectionate and he'd love you if you gave him a chance."

"No," Tania said fiercely, half turning away.

"Why not?" Mandy demanded. "He's . . ."

"Don't you see?" Tania cried, spinning around passionately. "If you love something you only lose it!" Her eyes searched Mandy's astonished face. "If you love nothing then you've got nothing to lose and nothing can hurt you ever again!" Her shoulders suddenly sagged. "Oh, what's the use?" she said bitterly. "How could *you* understand, anyway?" Turning abruptly she ran down the hill.

Mandy stared after her, feeling shocked. *Poor Tania,* she thought. *Imagine feeling like that.* She wondered what to do and had to admit that she didn't know the answer. Tania's feelings were a lot more complicated than she'd thought. Feeling uncomfortable, she turned and walked up the road toward Beacon House.

Mandy was quiet for the rest of the day. When she got home she worked hard in the clinic, trying to push the incident that afternoon to the back of her mind.

After the last patient had gone, Dr. Adam came over to her. "So, do you want to see my new exercise machine?"

"Has it arrived?" Mandy asked. All week they had been waiting for redelivery of Dr. Adam's package.

"It certainly has. Come and see."

Mandy followed him through to the house and into the living room. The air smelled of pine from the Christmas tree in the corner. "It's all over the place," she said, looking at the pieces of metal scattered on the floor.

Dr. Adam nodded. "There are instructions that tell you how to put it together."

"But you're not going to start now," Dr. Emily said, popping her head inside the door. "Dinner is almost ready."

"I'll just go and wash my hands," said Dr. Adam.

Mandy picked up the instructions. On one side it had a picture of the assembled machine with a tanned, muscular man in yellow Lycra shorts working out on it. "Do you think Dad will end up like that?" She grinned, showing the picture to her mom as they went into the kitchen together.

Dr. Emily laughed. "I doubt it." She took a closer look. "In fact, I hope not!"

After dinner, Mandy and Dr. Adam attempted to put

the machine together. "Now where does this piece fit?" he said, holding up an aluminum tube.

"I don't know," Mandy replied. She looked at the instructions and then at the half-constructed exercise machine in front of them. "We've got it wrong. We're going to have to start again."

Dr. Emily was sitting on the sofa, watching them, her legs curled underneath her. "I thought that the pamphlet says that this machine can be put together in five easy steps."

Mandy and Dr. Adam just looked at her. "These instructions just don't seem to make sense," Mandy said, turning the piece of paper around and looking at it from different angles. The phone rang and Dr. Adam, who was on call that night, got up to answer it.

"Here, let me see," Dr. Emily said to Mandy. She reached for the piece of paper and examined it thoughtfully. "Shouldn't you have attached that piece first?" she said, pointing to a piece of equipment. "Look." She got up from the sofa. "This is piece 'A.'"

Dr. Adam stuck his head in. "I've got to go to Drysdale Farm. They've got a horse down with colic." He glanced at the machine and coughed. "I'll, um, finish that when I get back."

As he left the room, Dr. Emily turned to Mandy. "This

doesn't look too difficult," she said, kneeling down beside her. "Now 'A' is going to connect to 'B' like this. You've just got to be logical. Pass me that piece over there. Come on, we can do this."

Mandy and Dr. Emily started assembling the machine. "So how were the horses today?" Dr. Emily asked as they worked.

Somewhat shamefaced, Mandy told her about Star escaping. "I should never have let go of the reins," she said. "But it all happened so quickly. Before I knew what was happening she was running off down the driveway."

"At least she's all right," Dr. Emily said comfortingly.

"Thanks to Tania," said Mandy. "If she hadn't been walking up the road then . . ." Her voice trailed off — she didn't like to think what might have happened if Tania hadn't been there to stop Star.

"How is Tania? Is your plan with Gabriel working?"

"Not very well," Mandy sighed.

Dr. Emily looked sympathetic. "I told you not to expect miracles. But maybe in a little while she'll come around."

Or maybe not, thought Mandy. She could still hear Tania's words from that afternoon. If you love something you only lose it, she had said. If she felt like that, then she was never going to let herself love Gabriel.

"Mandy?" Dr. Emily said, looking keenly at her. "Is something the matter?"

Normally, Mandy told her mom everything, but now she shook her head. "No, nothing," she said quickly. She didn't want to talk about that afternoon. She was sure that Tania wouldn't want her words repeated.

"Are you sure?" Dr. Emily persisted. "You were very quiet when you got back this afternoon."

"I'm sure!" Mandy met her mother's steady gaze. "Well, I *am* worried about Imogen," she said. It was really only a half-lie. She *was* feeling anxious about her and her new pony. "Star's a real handful. When we got back today Imogen rode her in the paddock, but she's very lively."

Dr. Emily appeared to accept the explanation. "Star's probably unsettled by the move and the change of rider," she said. "She's used to being ridden by an experienced twelve-year-old, and now she's suddenly got an inexperienced seven-year-old on her back and is deciding to act up and see what she can get away with. Ponies can be naughty like that. I think you'll find she settles down in time."

I hope so, thought Mandy. It was obvious how much Imogen loved her new pony, and it would be awful if Star proved too much for her to handle.

Dr. Emily sat back and looked at the fully assembled exercise machine. "There," she said, satisfied. "The instructions *were* correct. Five easy steps and it's assembled." Her eyes teased Mandy. "Now why couldn't you and your father do that?"

Seven

As Mandy and James biked up to Beacon House the next morning, Mandy told him about her mom putting the exercise machine together. "You should have seen Dad's face when he came in." She grinned. "He couldn't stop staring."

"Has he tried it out yet?" James said.

Mandy nodded. "He was going to do fifteen minutes before breakfast," she said.

"And?"

"He managed five!"

James grinned. "Maybe he'll build up gradually."

"Hmm," Mandy said, not convinced. "I think it was

harder work than he was expecting." They rode on a bit.

"Should we take Gabriel to Tania's this morning?" James asked.

"No." Mandy saw James look at her in surprise. "I . . . I don't think it's a good idea to take him there every day," she said, blushing slightly.

"Why not?" James said, astonished. "I thought that was the plan."

"I know but . . . well, she was a bit upset yesterday."

To her relief, James didn't ask any other questions. He just shrugged. "Okay."

"We could take him out for a little walk down the driveway though," Mandy suggested. "It would do him good to have some exercise."

Imogen was out visiting a friend that morning so Mandy and James caught Gabriel and walked him down the driveway. As they left, they could hear Star whinnying to him. He turned around and called back to her.

"I'm glad they're such good friends," Mandy said. They reached the road and let him graze on the grass at the side.

Mandy looked over the stone wall. From here, she could see the road as it wound its way down the hillside. She stiffened. Sitting on a wall, a bit farther down the road, was Tania. Mandy was about to draw back when Tania looked up and saw her. Feeling almost as if she had been spying, Mandy half raised her hand in an embarrassed wave. She moved back from the wall. She guessed Tania wanted to be alone.

But to her surprise, a few minutes later, Tania came walking around the corner toward them.

"It's Tania!" James said to Mandy. "Hi!" he called out.

Tania reached them. "Hi." Her cheeks were slightly flushed and she spoke quickly as if she had something that she wanted to get out. "Look, I'm . . . um . . . sorry about yesterday," she said, looking at Mandy. "I shouldn't have shouted at Imogen — or you."

Mandy felt very awkward. "That's all right," she muttered. "Forget it."

There was a silence. It seemed to go on forever. "Well . . . um . . . I better go," Tania said. "I guess that's all I came to say." Her shoulders sagged and she turned.

An impulse seized Mandy. "Tania!" she called. "We were just going to take Gabe for a walk. Why don't you come with us?" Tania hesitated. "Come on."

"Okay," Tania said with a shy smile. "Thanks."

They started up the road with James leading Gabriel. The little horse walked eagerly, his ears pricked. He seemed to love exploring new places.

"Where does this road lead to?" Tania asked, after a while.

"Up to the lighthouse. You should be able to see it soon," Mandy replied.

They passed some high hedges. "That's Upper Welford Hall," James told Tania. "Sam Western lives there. He's a big dairy farmer."

"Not a very nice one," said Mandy. She and James exchanged glances. The had experienced several unpleasant run-ins with Sam Western in the past.

"What about up there?" Tania asked, pointing up a dirt road.

"That's High Cross Farm," Mandy said. "Lydia Fawcett owns it. She keeps goats."

"And that's Piper's Wood," said James, pointing to some land that bordered Sam Western's land.

Gabriel pulled James over to a patch of grass and they stopped to let him graze. From their viewpoint they could see all the way down the valley. The town of Welford was nestled at the bottom. Mandy spotted the church, the Fox and Goose, and Animal Ark. "There's your house," she pointed out to Tania.

Tania stared for a long while and then suddenly shook her head. "I'm never going to get used to living here," she said, half to herself.

Mandy looked at Tania's unhappy face. "You will," she said. "Susan Collins moved here from London and she got used to it."

"But I don't *want* to get used to it!" Tania's voice grew passionate. "I hate it! I want to be in my old house with our swimming pool and stables. I want to be near my friends. I don't want to be here!" Tears welled up in her eyes. As if sensing her unhappiness, Gabriel stepped closer to her. Almost without thinking, Tania put a hand on his neck. "It's horrible not knowing anyone," she said. "I speak to my friends on the phone but it's not the same." She swallowed. "Nothing's the same."

"Do you see your dad much?" James asked.

Tania's face darkened. "Never. I hate him. He ruined my life." She wiped a tear from her cheek and turned abruptly. "I'd better go," she said.

"We'll come with you," Mandy said. "It's probably been a long enough walk for Gabe."

They started walking back down the road. *Poor Tania*, Mandy thought, glancing across. *It can't be easy for her. She must be so lonely not having any friends here.* An idea formed in her mind. "James and I are going Christmas shopping tomorrow morning," she said to Tania as they reached the Parker-Smythes' house. "We're meeting at nine-thirty. Would you like to come?"

Tania looked surprised. "You wouldn't mind?" she said, looking from Mandy to James.

"Of course not," James said.

Mandy grinned at her. "You'll have to put up with helping me choose socks for my granddad, though."

Tania almost smiled. "I guess I can cope." She looked Mandy straight in the eye. "Thanks," she said.

"We'll come for you!" Mandy called as Tania set off down the hill. "Nine-thirty, remember!"

"See you then!" Tania called back and Mandy noticed that her step seemed lighter than before.

Mandy came into the kitchen the following morning to find her dad reading the paper and drinking a cup of coffee. She raised her eyebrows. "Shouldn't you be using your exercise machine?"

Dr. Adam jumped rather guiltily to his feet. "Well, you know, there's a busy morning ahead. I don't really have time."

Mandy gave him a stern look. "You have to make time for exercise," she informed him. "Anyway, I thought that this machine was supposed to make exercise easy."

"Hmm," said Dr. Adam. He pulled on his white coat. "I think I'll just go and check the residential unit." He hurried out the door.

"I hope Tania's going to be in a good mood today," James said when he arrived a little later.

Mandy nodded. "Me, too. You didn't mind me asking her, did you?"

James shook his head. "It can't be much fun for her not having any friends here," he said. "Which stores should we go to first?" he asked, as they set off for Tania's house.

"How about Mr. Cecil's chocolate shop?" Mandy suggested. "I want to get Jean and Simon something from there."

James nodded. They reached Willow Cottage and knocked on the door. Tania opened it. "Hi," she said with a shy smile. "Come in. I'll just get my coat." James and Mandy stepped into the hall.

"Hello," said Sally Benster, coming in from the kitchen. "So, Tania tells me that you're all going Christmas shopping." Mandy and James nodded. "Well, have fun," Mrs. Benster said as Tania came running down the stairs with her coat.

The phone rang and Mrs. Benster hurried to pick it up.

"Come on," said Tania to Mandy and James. "Let's go."

"Tania!" Mrs. Benster called, as they were halfway out the door. "Hang on a minute!" She beckoned her over. "It's Dad."

Tania's face darkened. "I'm not speaking to him!"

"Tania," Mrs. Benster sighed. "He wants to come and visit before Christmas — to bring your Christmas presents over."

"I don't want any Christmas presents from him!" Tania exclaimed. "I'm not going to see him!"

"Tania!"

"No!" Tania turned and ran out the door. Mandy and James stood in the hallway, looking awkwardly after her. Mrs. Benster covered the receiver. "Sorry about that," she said to them quickly. "Look, have a nice time shopping. I'll sort this out with Tania when she gets back."

Mandy and James caught up with Tania at the end of the front yard. She was scowling fiercely and Mandy decided that it was better not even to try and talk about what had just happened. "The bus stop's this way," she said.

Once on the bus, Tania threw herself down in a seat and stared out the window. Mandy hoped Tania wasn't going to be in a bad mood all day. She looked at James. "So what are you getting for your mom?" she asked, trying to sound as normal as possible.

"A scarf," he said. "How about you?"

"I'm not sure yet, but I thought maybe some different kinds of aromatherapy oils."

To Mandy's relief, as the bus journey passed and she and James talked, the angry look started to fade from Tania's face. By the time they reached Walton she was sharing ideas for presents with them.

"I can't think of anything to get my grandma," she said. "She's hard to shop for and she gives me really weird presents. Last year she gave me a brown and pink wool hat and gloves and now, whenever I go to see her, I have to wear them!"

They went from store to store. The streets had been decorated with tinsel and strings of Christmas lights. There were people bustling everywhere and every store they went into was playing Christmas music. The festive atmosphere seemed to keep Tania in a good mood. The only dangerous moment was when Mandy and James started discussing the presents they were going to get for their dads.

Tania shook back her blond hair. "Well, I guess that's one good thing about my parents being divorced, I don't have to buy Dad a present." Her tone was light but Mandy saw the barely suppressed emotion in her eyes.

"Aren't you going to get him anything?" James asked.

Tania shook her head. "Nope. Why should I? If it hadn't been for him they would never have gotten divorced." She saw their curious faces. "He was always away on business. Mom says they grew apart." She frowned. "I know they could have made it work if they'd tried harder. I think Dad just didn't want to. If he'd really cared he could have stayed at home more."

Mandy had a feeling that things probably hadn't been

that simple, but she certainly wasn't going to risk annoying Tania by saying anything.

Tania's mouth was set in a thin line. "Dad's ruined everything for me," she said angrily. "He's ruined my life and I never want to speak to him again!"

"Umm, I think I'll just go in here," muttered James as they passed the hardware store.

Mandy thankfully followed him in. Tania's moods changed so quickly, it was difficult keeping up with her. But surely her father couldn't be as bad as she made out. Mandy had a feeling that it was just Tania's anger and not her real feelings talking.

By the time they got back on the bus they were all weighed down with bags full of presents. "I'm going to wrap mine tonight," Mandy said.

"I think I'll do mine this afternoon," Tania said. She sighed. "It's not like I've got anything else to do."

"What about coming with us to Imogen's?" James suggested.

Remembering Tania's reaction when she had seen Star two days before, Mandy was surprised when Tania said, "Okay." She looked warningly at them. "But I'm not helping with Star," she said. "She's Imogen's now."

As the bus chugged along the road toward Welford, Mandy thought about Imogen. How would she react

when she saw her cousin? She had been very upset after Tania had shouted at her and hadn't mentioned Tania's name since. Mandy crossed her fingers. She hoped everything would be all right.

When they arrived at the stables, they found Imogen grooming Star, with Mrs. Parker-Smythe helplessly holding a body brush in her manicured fingers. "You do her tail, Mommy," Imogen was saying.

Gabriel was tied up next to Star. As they came through the gate he turned and, pricking his tiny black ears, whinnied softly at them.

"Tania, darling!" Mrs. Parker-Smythe exclaimed. "What a lovely surprise."

Mandy looked at Imogen. The little girl was staring at Tania with a mixture of fear and anger in her eyes.

"Look who's here, Immi," Mrs. Parker-Smythe said, turning to her daughter.

Imogen glared at Tania. "Go away!"

Mrs. Parker-Smythe started in astonishment. "Immi?"

"I don't want her here, Mommy. Tell her to go away!" Imogen pleaded.

Tania stood looking very awkward, and her face went red.

"Imogen, what's the matter with you?" Mrs. Parker-Smythe said. "Now say hello to Tania nicely."

"No!" Throwing down the brush she was holding, Imogen burst into tears and ran off.

"I'll go after her!" Mandy said quickly. She caught up with Imogen by the gate. Tears were running down the little girl's face.

"I don't want Tania here!" she sobbed. "She thinks I shouldn't have Star. I hate her!"

Mandy put her arm around her. "But she's your cousin, Immi."

"I don't care!" Imogen sobbed.

"I know she shouted at you," Mandy said. "But she was upset." She squeezed Imogen's arm. "Come on, Immi. Imagine how you would feel if you had had to sell Star." To her relief Imogen's sobs quieted down.

"Well, she's not going to help me with Star," Imogen muttered at last.

"She won't," Mandy said and she led Imogen back over to the others.

"Immi!" said Mrs. Parker-Smythe. "Darling! How could you be so rude to Tania? Now say you're sorry."

"Sorry," Imogen muttered, not sounding as if she meant it. She turned to her mother. "I want to ride!" she said. "I want to ride Star in the paddock."

While Mandy and James helped her to tack up Star and Mrs. Parker-Smythe helped Imogen find her hat and gloves, Tania stood on her own by Gabriel. She tried to ignore him but he wouldn't let her, constantly trying to pull toward her and get at her pockets. When she moved out of his reach he pawed his front hoof on the ground until, finally, she had to go and stand beside him to keep him quiet. He seemed determined to make Tania like him.

At last, Star was ready and Imogen led her down to the paddock. James brought Gabriel down to the gate.

Tania came to stand beside him. Her eyes were fixed on Imogen and Star.

"Are you going to be all right?" Mandy asked Imogen as she mounted and Star threw her head up. Imogen nodded.

"Be careful, Immi!" Mrs. Parker-Smythe called nervously, as Mandy let go of the reins and Star pranced around the field. "Oh dear, Star looks a little too excited," she added.

Star jogged and pulled. Imogen kept her reins short and Star started to shake her head. Mandy glanced at Tania. Her eyes were agitated and suddenly, as if she couldn't bear to watch any longer, she turned and started adjusting Gabriel's blanket. He nuzzled her affectionately. She smoothed his forelock out from underneath his bridle. "There's a good boy," she murmured, her back to Imogen and Star. "Good boy."

Imogen walked and trotted Star around the paddock for fifteen minutes.

"Maybe you could give Imogen some lessons, Tania?" Mrs. Parker-Smythe said as Imogen brought Star in.

"I don't need lessons, Mommy," Imogen protested. "I'm fine!"

Mrs. Parker-Smythe looked doubtful. "I don't know. You didn't canter once. Maybe we should have gotten you a quieter pony."

"No!" Imogen exclaimed. "Star's perfect! I love her!"

"I know you do, sweetheart, but she is a bit of a handful."

"I can handle it!" Imogen turned to Mandy. "I can, can't I, Mandy?"

Mandy nodded. "I'm sure Star will settle down soon, Mrs. Parker-Smythe."

Imogen's mom looked at Star with a worried expression on her face. "Well, we'll see," she said, not sounding convinced. "Now give the reigns to James, Imogen, and come inside."

Imogen and James led Star and Gabriel down to the paddock. Mandy swallowed. Surely, Mrs. Parker-Smythe couldn't really be thinking about selling Star? It would break Imogen's heart. She caught sight of Tania watching the animals being released into the field. She knew Tania's feeling about not helping with Star but this was really important. It could mean the difference between Star staying and being sold. She hurried over. "Tania . . ." she began.

"No," Tania said abruptly before Mandy had even asked the question. "I'm not helping."

"Why not?" Mandy demanded.

"I just can't!"

"But why?"

Tania glared at her. "Just forget it, okay? I said no!" She strode off to stand at the paddock fence.

Mandy's heart sank. If Tania wouldn't help then she and James would have to think of something. And remembering the worried look on Mrs. Parker-Smythe's face, she had a feeling they were going to have to think of something fast!

Eight

"If Star *is* too much for Imogen, it might be better for her to be sold," Dr. Emily said when Mandy told her the problem that evening.

"Mom!" said Mandy.

"You've got to be realistic, sweetheart. Imogen would probably be happier with a quieter pony." Dr. Emily put out a cheese and onion quiche on the table.

"She wouldn't. She loves Star!" Mandy refused to believe that Imogen would be better off with a different pony. Yes, Star was lively but deep down Mandy was sure she was a loving, affectionate pony who just needed time to settle into her new home. She had behaved beautifully when Tania had stopped her from running down the road and had calmed her down.

Mandy hoped James would have some ideas of what they could do to help Imogen with Star, but when he arrived at Animal Ark the next morning he was also at a loss. "I guess we've just got to make sure that Mrs. Parker-Smythe doesn't see her doing anything wrong," he said. "And that she does settle down eventually."

Mandy agreed. "If only Tania would step in."

"Even if she would, do you think Imogen would accept her help?" James said. "Tania isn't exactly her favorite person at the moment."

Mandy sighed. She had to admit that James was right. *Oh, why is life never simple?* she thought.

To Mandy's surprise, Tania turned up at the stables that morning. "I was bored," she said by way of explanation. She sat on the fence and watched them start to groom Star and Gabriel. Imogen completely ignored her.

"You could help if you wanted," Mandy suggested to Tania, as she picked up a body brush.

Tania shook her head. "No thanks." She watched James brushing out Gabriel's tail. "You'll break the hairs like that," she said as he dragged the brush through the tangles. "Look, you do it like this." Jumping off the fence, she showed him how to untangle a few hairs at a time. "It takes longer but it's worth it," she told him.

"Thanks," he said.

She moved around to Gabriel's head and patted him. "You don't want broken hairs in your tail, do you?" she said gently to him, and Mandy saw her reach into her pocket and feed him a piece of carrot. Mandy raised her eyebrows slightly but knew better than to risk annoying Tania by making a comment.

Imogen got Star's tack. "Will you help me, James?" she asked, holding out the bridle. As usual, Star started to shake her head as soon as James tried to put the bridle on. At last, he got it over her ears and started to buckle up the straps. Star carried on shaking her head.

Tania frowned from the fence. "The browband's too tight," she said. The others turned and looked at her. She shrugged. "It is. It's new, isn't it?"

Imogen nodded. The browband on the bridle was brand-new from the saddlers, made of leather and covered with blue and red velvet.

"Well, it's too tight," said Tania. "Star's got a broad forehead and needs a bigger browband than most ponies. If you change it she'll stop shaking her head so much." She looked as if that was her final word.

"Have you got the old browband?" Mandy asked Imogen. She told them it was in the house, and hurried off to get it.

James held Star. She stamped her feet impatiently. "It will help calm her down if you walk her around before you put the saddle on," Tania said. "I used to walk her before getting on. It seems to settle her."

Mandy felt exasperation fill her. "For goodness sake, Tania. Why don't you just agree to help?"

Tania jumped off the fence and walked to the paddock gate. She stared out at the field, her face stormy.

Mandy only just managed to control her temper.

James touched her arm. "Star's ready. Are you coming?"

Mandy nodded. They left Tania by the paddock gate and took Gabriel and Star out along the driveway and up the hill. Having Gabriel walking alongside her seemed to calm Star down. Imogen was very happy. "Star's being much better today," she said, patting her pony's neck. "Mommy should see her like this."

When they got back to the stables, Gabriel lifted his head and whinnied to Tania. She turned from the gate, looking surprised and almost pleased. She came over. "Hi," she said. She patted the Miniature horse, who nudged her with his head. Her bad mood seemed to have vanished. "How were they both?"

"Not too bad," said Mandy.

"Do you want me to take him down to the field?" Tania asked James, who was holding Gabriel's lead rope.

"Okay." James nodded.

Mandy watched Tania lead Gabriel off and sighed to herself. Being with Tania was very wearing. You just never knew what mood she would be in. It was like walking on eggshells, she thought, always going carefully, never knowing when she would crack.

Mandy, James, and Tania walked back to the town together at lunchtime. Mrs. Benster was in the yard of Willow Cottage, collecting some logs from a pile by the back door.

"Hi, Mom!" Tania called.

Mrs. Benster smiled. "What good timing. I just made some apple pie. Would you like some?"

"Yes, please," Mandy and James said eagerly. They followed her into the house.

"Tania, something came for you in the mailbox," Mrs. Benster said, handing out the apple pie. "It's over there, on the side."

Mandy saw that Tania suddenly looked suspicious. "It's not from Dad is it?"

Mrs. Benster sighed. "No."

Tania picked up the brown envelope and started to open it.

"What is it?" James asked, munching on his warm pie.

Tania pulled out a small cardboard folder from the envelope. "Miniature Horse Passport," she read out loud. She quickly flipped through it. "It's a passport for Gabriel."

Mandy remembered. "It must have been forwarded by the post office," she said. "Dad said they had Gabe's passport there." Tania handed it over to her and she looked through the pages. There was an identification page with a photograph of Gabriel and details such as his height, color, a record of his breeding, a page showing his vaccinations, and then a page about the details of the owner. "Look!" she said to Tania. "It's got your name in it!"

Tania looked. "'Owner: Tania Benster,'" she read out loud. "'Address: Willow Cottage, 16 Walton Road, Welford.'"

"Wow," James said, looking over her shoulder. "Doesn't it look good?"

For a few minutes Tania stared down at the page and then she abruptly put the passport down. "It will have to be changed," she said. "He's not mine."

"Yes, he is," Mandy pointed out. "It says so. You're his owner."

"But I don't want to be," said Tania, almost desper-

ately. She pushed the passport across the table and turned to her mom. "You'll have to send it back and get it changed, Mom. Tell them he's not mine."

"Well, we'll see," Mrs. Benster said.

"No, Mom! You will!"

Mrs. Benster held up her hands. "All right," she said. "I'm in no mood for an argument." She went over to the stove and turned it on. "Your father's coming over tomorrow afternoon, Tania. He wants to see you."

Tania stared in horror. "No!"

"Yes," Mrs. Benster said. She looked firmly at her daughter. "I said you'd be in."

"Well, I won't be!" Tania exclaimed, her eyes blazing. "I'm not going to see him. I hate him!" With that she stormed out of the room, slamming the door behind her.

There was a silence. Mandy glanced at Mrs. Benster. Her face looked suddenly very tired. As if suddenly remembering that Mandy and James were there, she turned to them. "I'm sorry," she said. "I should have told Tania when she didn't have company." She ran a hand across her forehead. "Sometimes I think all my common sense has deserted me."

Mandy stood up a little awkwardly. "We better go," she said.

James nodded. "Can you tell Tania we'll see her tomorrow morning?"

Mrs. Benster nodded and showed them to the door.

As Mandy and James biked up to Beacon House, the air froze their breath in great white clouds. It had turned much colder and they were very happy to have their gloves and scarves.

"You better ride Star in the paddock today," Mandy told Imogen. "The road will be too icy."

As Imogen mounted, Tania arrived. She came down to the paddock and leaned against the fence. Gabriel, who had been grazing, came over and nudged her hands hopefully. Did you bring me any treats today? he seemed to say.

"I'm going to canter Star," Imogen told Mandy and James. "Mommy thinks I'm too scared to, but I'm going to show her that I'm not."

She rode off. Mandy and James watched her trotting around. "I don't know if cantering is such a good idea," Mandy said to James.

Star was pulling hard but Imogen looked determined. After a few minutes, she grabbed hold of Star's mane, leaned forward, and kicked hard with her heels. Star leaped forward, throwing her head between her knees and pulling the reins free from Imogen's hands. With a frightened cry, Imogen tumbled from the saddle. For one awful moment there was a tangle of legs and arms and hooves, and then Imogen was lying on the grass and Star was cantering away.

"Quick!" Mandy gasped to James.

They scrambled over the gate and started racing across the field. To her relief, Mandy saw Imogen starting to sit up. But her relief was short-lived. A high-pitched shriek rang out behind them. Mandy turned around. Mrs. Parker-Smythe was standing at the paddock gate, her eyes wide with horror.

Imogen stood up. She looked shaky but appeared to be all in one piece.

"Are you all right?" James gasped.

Imogen nodded. "I fell off," she said dazedly.

"We saw," said James.

"And so did your mom," said Mandy in dismay, seeing Mrs. Parker-Smythe running across the field toward them.

Mrs. Parker-Smythe reached them and clasped Imogen in her arms. "Oh, Immi, are you all right, sweetheart?" she exclaimed.

"I'm fine, Mommy," Imogen said, trying to wriggle out of her mother's embrace. "I just fell off, that's all."

"Just fell off! I saw what that pony did. I was watching from the house. That's it, Immi. Enough's enough. That pony has to go!"

"No!" Imogen cried, aghast.

"Yes," Mrs. Parker-Smythe said firmly. "I'm not having you risking your neck. Star needs a more experienced rider and you need a pony you can take out on rides and canter around on and jump. Star's too lively."

"But I love her!" wailed Imogen.

"I won't hear another word on the subject!" Mrs. Parker-Smythe said.

"I hate you!" Imogen cried, her face scrunched up, and then, turning, she ran across the field toward the house. Mrs. Parker-Smythe hurried after her.

"Well," said James in a stunned voice. "Poor Imogen."

Mandy turned to Tania, who was standing near them, holding Star. "Tania," she pleaded. "You've got to help. You heard what your aunt said. She's going to sell Star. If you say you'll help Imogen she might change her mind."

Tania's lip trembled. "I can't."

"You can!" Mandy exclaimed, but Tania shook her head stubbornly. It was too much for Mandy. She lost her temper. "For goodness sake, will you stop being so selfish?" she cried. "Why don't you try thinking about someone other than yourself for a change?" She saw the shock on Tania's face but went on regardless, her anger with Tania fueled by her concern for Imogen and Star and her pent-up frustration. "You don't think about anyone else's feelings. Everyone's going out of their way to be nice to you but you don't care about anyone but yourself."

Tania stood up tall, her eyes blazing fiercely. "You don't know what it's like to have your parents get divorced!"

"No, I don't!" Mandy exclaimed equally fiercely. "But I do know that it doesn't give you the right to go around hurting other people." With that, she grabbed Star from Tania and marched toward the gate.

"Mandy!" James said, hurrying after her, sounding shocked. "Calm down."

She shook his hand off her arm and walked on, but it wasn't long before her temper began to cool. By the time she reached the gate, her hands were starting to tremble. *Oh no*, she thought. *What have I done?* She fumbled with the bolt.

James pulled back the gate for her. But just as Mandy started to lead Star inside they heard a sob. They turned around. Tania had collapsed into a heap on the ground and was crying into her hands.

James glanced at Mandy with worried eyes. "What should we do?"

Mandy swallowed. "Go back." It was the only thing they could do.

James nodded. With a nervous feeling in the pit of her stomach, Mandy started to walk Star slowly back across the field toward Tania.

"Look!" James whispered suddenly.

Gabriel was walking toward Tania. He stopped beside her and then started nuzzling at her hair. Tania tried to push him away. "Go away!" she gulped, but

Gabriel wouldn't leave. He nuzzled her face and hands. His affection was too much for Tania. A loud sob tore from her. "Oh, Gabe!" she cried, putting her arms around him. "No one understands. No one cares."

Mandy suddenly felt awful. She took a step forward. "Tania?" Tania jumped and looked up. For a second the two girls just stared at each other, then Mandy took a deep breath. "I'm sorry," she said. "I . . . I shouldn't have said those things."

For a moment, Mandy thought that Tania was going to explode at her again but then suddenly she bit her lip, and a tear trickled down her cheek. "No, I'm the one who should be sorry," she whispered, her voice trembling. "I have been selfish. I know I have." She brushed her tears away with the back of her hand. "It's just so hard not to be." Her voice took on a note of despair. "It feels like no one cares."

"Gabe cares," James said quietly, looking at the little horse who was nuzzling Tania.

Tania touched Gabriel's nose. His lips nibbled gently at her fingers.

"It doesn't matter how many times you push him away," Mandy said. "He'll always come back. That's the good thing about animals. They're always there for you."

James nodded. "They love you, no matter what."

Tania looked at Gabe. "He's yours," Mandy said to her. "And he loves you."

Tania's eyes looked panicky. "But I don't want him to love me," she said.

Mandy understood. "In case you lose him?"

Tania nodded.

"But that won't happen." Mandy kneeled down beside her. "Don't you understand? You're his owner, Tania. It says so on the passport. No one can take him away from you. He's yours." She looked pleadingly at the other girl. "He'll love you so much if you just give him a chance."

As if he agreed, Gabriel snorted gently and nuzzled Tania's hair. Mandy saw Tania's face melt. "Oh, Gabe," she whispered and she flung her arms around his neck again. Tears ran down her cheeks. "You *are* mine, aren't you? All mine!"

Mandy looked at James in relief.

At last, Tania stood up. There were still traces of tears on her face but her eyes were brave. "I'm going to tell Aunt Sonia that I'll help with Star," she said. "You're right. I have been selfish. But not anymore."

"Tania!" cried Mandy. "That's great! I'm sure if you offer to help, Imogen will be allowed to keep her."

Tania took a deep breath and looked at Star. "It'll be hard," she said. "I do still love her. But she'll be happy with Imogen." She put her hand on Gabriel's neck. "And I've got Gabriel now." She looked toward the Parker-Smythes' house. "Here goes!"

"Maybe you should let your aunt calm down a little first," James suggested.

Mandy nodded, remembering Mrs. Parker-Smythe's horrified face. "We could come back after lunch," she said. "We don't want to ask her when she's still really upset. She might say no."

Tania saw the sense in what they were saying. "Okay," she said. "But right after lunch."

They went back to Tania's house for lunch. She showed them around the backyard. It wasn't huge but it was securely fenced in with two solid-looking sheds. "This will be perfect for Gabe," Mandy said.

"One shed for him to live in and one for his feed and bedding," said Tania. "And I'll take him up to visit Star a lot so they can still stay friends."

Tania showed them her bedroom. It had bare white walls and most of her things were still in boxes. Tania went happily to the window. "I'll be able to see Gabe from here." She looked around the room. "I guess I should really start putting some of my posters up and unpacking my things."

Mandy smiled. She hoped that it was a sign that Tania was finally starting to accept that her life had changed.

After grabbing a sandwich they hurried back up the hill eager to find Mrs. Parker-Smythe and Imogen. It was getting very cold and by the time they reached Beacon House they all had bright red cheeks and noses.

"It's going to snow!" said Mandy, looking at the sky. "I bet it's going to snow."

"We can go sledding," James said. "Do you like sledding?" he asked Tania.

"I love it," she replied. "But I haven't got a sled."

"You can share ours then," James said.

"Thanks!" Tania looked really happy. She reached for the doorbell. "Well, here goes," she said. They stamped their feet in the cold as they waited for someone to answer. The housekeeper, Mrs. Bates, eventually opened the door.

"Hi, Mrs. Bates," Tania said. "We're looking for Aunt Sonia."

"She's gone out," the housekeeper told them.

"Oh." Tania's face fell. "Is Imogen here then?" she asked.

Mrs. Bates shook her head. "No, she went out to the stables about half an hour ago."

"Oh, right," said Tania. "Well, okay, we'll go and find her there."

They went around to the stables. "Imogen!" Tania called out.

There was no answer. They checked the stables and then walked down to the field. Gabriel was standing by the gate. "Where's Star?" Mandy asked in surprise. The two were normally always together.

"Mandy!" said James, looking around the field. "She's not here!"

Mandy frowned. "But she's got to be!"

"Let's check the tack room," Tania said. They ran to the tack room. Star's saddle and bridle were gone. In their place was a note.

"'Dear Mommy,'" Mandy read out loud, grabbing it. "'I have taken Star out for a ride. I want to show you that I can. She is safe, really she is. See you later.'" Mandy looked up. "Love, Imogen."

"Oh, no," Tania whispered. "What if she falls off again?"

"And this time really hurts herself," said James.

"We've got to find her," Mandy said, throwing down the note. "Before it's too late."

Nine

They ran as fast they could down the driveway. "She must have gone up toward High Cross!" James panted. "We would have seen her if she'd been coming down the hill."

Mandy slid and almost fell as she stepped on a patch of ice. Her heart lurched. What if Star was to slip and stumble? She felt sick to her stomach thinking of the lively pony and of Imogen, the inexperienced rider.

Tania suddenly stopped dead. Mandy and James almost ran into her. "Listen!" she exclaimed.

Mandy heard a faint clatter of hooves. It got louder and louder. "Star!" she gasped as the palomino pony came cantering down the driveway toward them. She was riderless, her reins flapping around her legs.

Tania leaped in front of her. "Whoa!" The pony skidded to a halt and Tania grabbed her reins, her face pale. "Imogen must have fallen off," she said.

"We've got to find her!" said Mandy. "She might be hurt, and it's so cold." As she spoke, the first few flakes of snow started to fall.

Tania seemed to make up her mind. Putting her foot in the stirrup she mounted the excited pony. Star shook her head and twirled on the spot.

"What are you doing?" Mandy cried, as Tania turned the pony back down the driveway.

"Going to find Imogen. It'll be quicker this way. I can retrace her tracks."

"But . . ."

Tania didn't listen. She kicked her heels into Star's side and the pony galloped away, keeping to the grass at the side of the driveway.

"Oh, no!" gasped Mandy to James. "Look!"

Mrs. Parker-Smythe's sleek silver car was turning in through the gates. Mrs. Parker-Smythe slammed her brakes to avoid Star and jumped out of the car. "Tania! What are you doing?"

Tania galloped past without replying. Mandy and James ran up to Mrs. Parker-Smythe. "What on earth's going on?" Mrs. Parker-Smythe demanded. "What is Tania —"

Mandy interrupted her with a hurried explanation. "Imogen's taken Star out. We think she must have fallen off somewhere. Tania's gone to find her."

Mrs. Parker-Smythe stared at her uncomprehendingly. "Imogen took Star out on a ride? On her own?"

"Yes! There's a note in the tack room. She said she wanted to prove to you that she could." Mandy made a split-second decision to tell Mrs. Parker-Smythe everything.

As the words sank in, Mandy saw Mrs. Parker-Smythe go pale. "Oh, my goodness," she whispered.

"We've got to help Tania look for Imogen," said Mandy. "Now!"

She ran out of the gate, ignoring Mrs. Parker-Smythe's cry of "Wait!"

"This way," said James, turning up the hill. They ran past Upper Welford Hall and past the driveway to High Cross Farm. Snowflakes swirled toward them and their feet slipped on the road. Every so often, there was a set of hoofprints on the grass at the side of the road but they were quickly becoming covered with a dusting of white. "Which way now?" gasped James, as the road ended by forking into two rough paths. One led up to the Beacon. One went around the side of the mountain and to Piper's Wood.

"This way!" said Mandy, spotting a trail of hoofprints. She ran along the narrow path pushing branches out of the way, tripping over hidden tree roots. The mud under the trees was so churned up that it was soon impossible to follow the hoofprints any farther. She stopped and looked around. What now? Paths led off in different directions, and the only sound was their gasping for breath. The snow was getting heavier now.

"Imogen!" called James. "Tania!"

His voice was loud in the eerie silence of the cold woods.

"Imogen!" Mandy shouted as loud as she could.

There was no reply. "Come on, we can't just wait here," Mandy said, running off down the widest of the paths.

They walked down the path, taking turns shouting out Imogen's name. Suddenly, James grabbed Mandy's arm. "Listen."

There was an answer, and then Tania came trotting through the trees. "Have you found her?" Mandy gasped as Tania dismounted.

Tania shook her head. "No. I lost the trail." She looked around at the dark trees, her eyes desperate. "She could be anywhere."

"We'll find her," Mandy said. "Come on!" They set off down the path again.

Tania led Star. "If only she could help us," she said as they reached a clearing and were faced with another four different paths.

Mandy looked at Star. The pony's ears were pricked. "Maybe she can!" she said. "Look at her! She's looking down that path."

"She might just have heard something," said Tania.

"Come on." James made the decision. "Let's go that way!"

"Imogen! Imogen!" they shouted, as they ran along. Suddenly, they heard a faint cry.

"That's her!" gasped Tania. "Come on!" They hurried along the path. As they called out, they heard her answer.

"We're closer!" said Mandy. They ran around a bend in the path and stopped. There was Imogen. She was huddled underneath an oak tree, tears streaming down her face. Snow had settled all around her.

"Oh, Immi!" cried Tania, flinging Star's reins at James and racing over to her cousin. "Are you all right?" Dropping to her knees, she wrapped her arms tightly around Imogen. "There, there. Don't cry. We're here now."

For a long moment Imogen just clung onto Tania.

Tears streamed down both their faces. "We've been so worried," said Tania.

"What happened, Imogen? Are you all right?" Mandy asked, kneeling down in the snow beside her.

Imogen took a deep gulping breath. "Star ran away with me. Something frightened her when we came into the woods and she just took off. I tried to stay on. It was horrible. There were branches hitting me and then she stumbled and I lost my grip. I . . . I hurt my ankle." Her voice rose. "And now Mommy's never going to let me keep Star!"

"She will," Tania said firmly. "I'm going to tell her I'll help you, Imogen. I'll come every day."

"Really?" said Imogen her face lighting up, full of hope.

"Really," said Tania. She hugged Imogen. "I'm sorry I've been so awful. But I'll help you from now on, I promise. I'll show you how to get Star to canter and I'll teach you how to jump. And when you're really good," she smiled, "Gabe and I will come and watch you at all the horse shows you're going to enter."

Imogen smiled happily. "I'd like that."

"Good," said Tania. She looked anxiously at Mandy. "But first we have to get you home."

"Let me have a look at your ankle," Mandy said. She tried to help Imogen off with her boot but the pain was too great for the little girl and she screamed. "We'd better leave it," Mandy said. "We need to get you back as quickly as possible."

"But I can't walk," said Imogen.

"You can sit on Star and we'll lead you," Mandy replied.

Looking slightly scared but determined, Imogen let Mandy and James help her onto Star's back. Her ankle knocked against the saddle and she gasped and went pale. For a second, Mandy thought she was going to faint.

"You're being very brave," she told Imogen. "Now come on, it won't be long before you're home."

They set off slowly down the path with Tania leading Star and Mandy and James walking on either side. Mandy looked anxiously at Imogen. She was starting to shiver. Mandy took off her jacket. "Here," she said. "Put this on, Imogen."

"But you'll get cold," Imogen said.

"No, I won't. I'm going to run ahead and try to get help," said Mandy. She looked at Tania and James, who both nodded. "See you later!" Mandy called, heading off into the trees.

She ran as fast as she could, her heart pounding in her throat, her breath coming in great gasps. At last, she reached Beacon House and banged on the door.

"Mandy!" cried Mrs. Parker-Smythe, opening it almost immediately. "Where's Imogen? Have you found her?"

"Yes!" Mandy gasped, struggling for breath. "She's in the woods. She hurt her ankle. James and Tania are with her."

Just then, there was the sound of a car driving up behind her. Mandy turned. "Dad!" she cried, seeing her father's Land Rover.

Dr. Adam leaped out. "I came as soon as I could," he said to Mrs. Parker-Smythe. He turned to Mandy. "What's happened? Have you found Imogen?"

"She's in the woods, with James and Tania. She hurt her ankle," Mandy said. "I said I'd get help."

"Okay, let's go," said Dr. Adam.

"Thank you so much for coming, Dr. Adam," said Mrs. Parker-Smythe, as they drove up the road in the Land Rover. "I just didn't know who else to call. My husband is away on business."

"No problem," said Dr. Adam, his eyes fixed on the snowy road. "Here we are."

Just as they threw open the doors of the Land Rover, Tania and James appeared, leading Imogen on Star.

"Immi!" cried Mrs. Parker-Smythe.

"Mommy!" Imogen cried and then she fainted.

*   *   *

"I don't think it's broken," said Dr. Adam a little while later, looking up from examining Imogen's ankle. It was so swollen that he had to cut through her riding boot to get it off. "I think it's just a bad sprain but you should visit the hospital just in case. I'll bandage it up until you get there."

Mandy, James, and Tania were sitting on towels on an enormous sofa. Everything in the Parker-Smythes' house seemed to be white and gold and Mandy was very conscious of her muddy jeans.

Imogen was wrapped in a blanket, with a cup of hot chocolate in her hands. Although she was safely back home she still looked anxious.

As Dr. Adam got to work, Mrs. Parker-Smythe looked gratefully at him. "Thank you so much, Adam."

Dr. Adam secured the bandage. "No problem," he said.

"I just don't understand why you did it, Immi," Mrs. Parker-Smythe said, turning to her daughter.

"Because you said you were going to sell Star. I wanted to show you that she was safe to ride!" Imogen replied.

"Well, she obviously isn't," said Mrs. Parker-Smythe. "She is going to have to go."

"No, Mommy!"

"Aunt Sonia," Tania broke in. "What if I help Immi? I could come here every day."

Mrs. Parker-Smythe shook her head. "Star's just too lively, Tania. I think Imogen needs a quieter pony."

"But I want Star!" Imogen cried.

"Star's fine," Tania protested. "She's only lively when you first get on. If I ride her each day before Imogen then she'll be as quiet as anything."

"But what if you're not here, Tania?"

"Well, I can show Imogen how to use a lunge rope," Tania said. "That would work just as well. But I will be here. I promise I'll come every day."

"We'll share her," Imogen said. "Like I share Button and Barney with John. Only it will be better because we'll look after her together and Tania won't have to go away to school like John does." She turned to Tania. "You can teach me how to jump."

Tania smiled. "And you can help me look after Gabe."

Mrs. Parker-Smythe looked shocked. "You've decided you want to keep Gabriel?" she said.

Tania nodded. "Thank you for buying him for me. I'm sorry I've been so horrible." She got up and hugged her aunt. "He's the best present I could ever have."

"Well, goodness," Mrs. Parker-Smythe said, blushing but hugging Tania back. "This is a surprise. What made you change your mind?"

Tania grinned at Mandy and James. "Oh, just an argument I had."

"An argument? Really, Tania, darling, you aren't making any sense!"

Tania looked at her aunt. "You will let Imogen keep Star, won't you?" she pleaded. "I really do promise I'll help, and I'll never let Imogen do anything dangerous. After all, Star did help us find Imogen. She showed us the right path to take in the woods."

"Please, Mommy!" Imogen said. "If it hadn't been for Star I might still be there now!"

Mrs. Parker-Smythe looked from one to the other and then nodded. "All right then."

"Oh, thank you, Mommy!" cried Imogen. Mandy breathed a huge sigh of relief.

"Now, young lady," Dr. Adam said to Imogen. "It's time to get you to the hospital." He bent down to pick her up.

"Please can I see Star and Gabriel before I go?" Imogen begged.

Dr. Adam looked at Mrs. Parker-Smythe, who nodded. "But not until you've put another coat on, and gloves and a hat," she said.

When Imogen was dressed to her mother's satisfaction, Dr. Adam lifted her up in his strong arms and carried her down to the stable. The snow had stopped falling and lay in a perfect white layer.

Star was in her loose box and Gabriel was in the shelter in the field. "I'll bring him in," Tania said quickly. "It's too cold for him out there. He'd better stay in a stable tonight and then tomorrow I'll take him down to my house."

"But you will bring him back a lot, won't you?" Imogen asked.

Tania nodded. "I promise."

As she went to get him, everyone else gathered around Star's stable door. Imogen stroked her gently on the nose. "I love you, Star," she whispered.

Just then, there was the sound of a car arriving. Mrs. Parker-Smythe looked up in surprise. "Who can that be?" she said. A tall man and a blond woman came around the side of the house.

"It's Tania's mom!" said James.

"Sally!" exclaimed Mrs. Parker-Smythe. Her tone changed slightly. "And . . . um . . . Richard."

Sally Benster looked around at everyone. "Hello," she said. "We're looking for Tania." She frowned. "She was supposed to be back at Willow Cottage."

Mandy looked at the man beside Mrs. Benster and her eyes suddenly widened as she remembered Mrs. Benster warning Tania that she wanted her to be at home that afternoon. Could this man be . . .

"Dad!" Everyone turned. Tania stood a little way off with Gabriel. She was staring at the man, her face pale.

Her father took a step forward. "Tania."

Tension hung in the freezing air as Tania and her father stared at each other. For a moment no one moved and then Gabe, curious as always, pulled forward to meet the stranger. Slipping on the snow, Tania let go of the lead rope. Gabe trotted over. "Nice pony," Mr. Benster said.

Mandy saw Tania redden. "He's mine and he's not a pony, he's a Miniature horse." She clicked her tongue. "Gabe!" The little horse looked around and then trotted back to her. She put her hand on his neck. "He's all mine." Her voice shook slightly on the last words as she stared almost defiantly at her father.

Gabriel stepped toward Mr. Benster.

"Gabe!" Tania called.

The little horse stopped and looked around at her. He pricked his ears as if to say, Well, what are you waiting for?

Tania looked at her dad and suddenly caught her breath in a sob.

"Tania," Mr. Benster said in concern.

The next instant, Tania was in her father's arms. "Oh, Dad!" she cried, her shoulders shaking as he pulled her close. Not wanting to be left out, Gabe tried to push in on the action. Tania started to half laugh and half cry. "Oh, Gabe, I do love you! And, Dad, I love you, too!"

"I love you, too, sweetheart," said Mr. Benster, hugging her as if he was never going to let her go. "No matter what happens. I always will!"

Mandy saw Mrs. Benster watching from a distance, tears spilling down her cheeks.

Oh, Gabe, Mandy thought. *You really are a wonderful horse.*

She felt her father touch her arm. "I think we might leave the Bensters here and get Imogen to the hospital," he said quietly. "Okay?"

Mandy nodded. "Okay," she said with a happy smile.

The Ambassador
of
Good Will

Ten

The next morning, when Mandy woke up at the usual time, her room felt colder and darker than normal and there was a strange stillness that hung in the air. She sat up quickly. The snow! How deep was it now?

Jumping out of bed, she raced to the window. "Oh, wow!" she gasped. Although the light was dim and gray, she could see that everything was covered in a thick, snowy blanket. The wheelbarrow in the garden, the flower beds, the bird table, the trees — everything was white.

Mandy felt her toes start to tingle from the cold. Excitement bubbled up in her. It had snowed and it was

Christmas Eve! Putting on some clothes, she hurried downstairs and went outside. The yard stretched out before her, an expanse of perfect whiteness. Mandy raced across it, leaving great snowy footprints. She stopped and grinned as she decided to test the snow by making a snowball.

Hearing the slight crunch of a footstep behind her, she turned around just in time to duck as a snowball flew past her ear. Dr. Adam was standing by the back door, another snowball already in his hands.

"Dad!" Mandy threw the snowball she was holding at him. Two minutes later, snowballs were flying back and forth across the yard and the still air was shattered by shrieks and shouts.

"Stop! Stop! I've got snow down my boots!" Mandy exclaimed at last.

"Count yourself lucky — it's down my neck!" Dr. Adam replied. Dusting off his hands he came over and put his arm around her. "It's a white Christmas."

Mandy nodded. "We can go sledding!"

"It doesn't look like much else will be happening to-day," Dr. Emily said, opening the side gate and looking at the snow that covered the driveway. "It's not going to be easy to get out in this."

Mandy suddenly remembered. "But James and I were

supposed to be helping Tania with Gabe," she said. "We were going to take him down to Willow Cottage."

"You'll find it difficult getting to Tania's in this," Dr. Emily said. "You'll have to wait until the roads have been cleared."

"I guess so." Mandy felt disappointed. She had been looking forward to seeing Gabriel finally settled into Tania's backyard.

Dr. Emily was already cooking breakfast as they went into the kitchen. She smiled as they came in, shaking the snow off their clothes. "You look like snowmen!" she said. "Now, who wants scrambled eggs on toast?"

Dr. Adam sighed happily. "A double helping, please!"

As Mandy watched her father dig into an enormous plateful of fluffy scrambled eggs, she grinned. "Seeing as you'll be stuck around here today, Dad, you'll be able to spend lots of time on your exercise machine!"

Dr. Adam froze with a mouthful of scrambled eggs halfway to his mouth.

"That's an excellent idea, Mandy," Dr. Emily said approvingly. She looked at Dr. Adam. "After all, Adam, you have been saying that the only reason you haven't been using it is because we've been so busy. Well, now's your chance."

Dr. Adam coughed. "Well, you know the clinic could use cleaning up."

"I'll do that," said Mandy helpfully.

"And the shelves could use organizing."

"I'll do that as well," Mandy said.

Dr. Adam thought for a moment. "There's all the paperwork," he said.

"Leave it for Jean," said Dr. Emily. "This is beginning to sound suspiciously like a list of excuses," she said, her green eyes twinkling as she tucked a strand of hair behind her left ear and looked at her husband.

"Dad!" said Mandy, pretending to sound shocked. "Surely you're not going to tell us that you are trying to get out of using your brand-new exercise machine? The machine that makes exercising effortless and easy."

Dr. Adam gave up the pretense. "It lied," he said.

"Poor Dad," Mandy said, putting her arm around him. "But you know what they say. No pain, no gain. Now, come on, let's get you into those sweats."

Dr. Adam was about to get up when his face suddenly brightened. "But I can't exercise right after breakfast, can I?" He shook his head. "It could be dangerous." He sat back firmly in his chair. "No, no, no. I'd better just sit here and read this magazine until my breakfast has been digested." He picked up his magazine with a contented sigh. "Are there any more eggs?" he asked, looking up hopefully.

By mid-morning, Mandy had cleaned the clinic and cleaned out and fed her rabbits and the animals in the residential unit. There didn't seem to be much else to do. The driveway and road were still far too deep in snow for her to go out.

She finished wrapping her Christmas presents and then called Tania. There was no answer. She called James to find that he was snowed in as well.

"Blackie loves it!" he said. "He's been racing around the yard all morning."

They arranged to go sledding as soon as the snow had been plowed. Mandy put down the phone and sighed. Although it was great that it had snowed, it wasn't much fun on her own.

She decided to go and check the driveway again to see if the snow had melted at all. She pulled on her boots and went outside. As she shut the door, she suddenly heard a faint noise and stopped to listen. It sounded like the tinkling of tiny bells. She frowned. What could it be? It seemed to be coming from down the driveway and it was getting louder. She waded through the snow and suddenly gasped in amazement. There, coming up the hill, were Tania and Gabriel. The

Miniature horse was pulling a red sled and sitting on it
was Imogen.

"Mandy!" the little girl cried, waving wildly.

"Hi!" Tania called out, who had snow almost up to the
top of her boots, but was grinning broadly.

"What are you doing here?" Mandy cried in delight as
they reached her. Imogen was covered in rugs and blan-
kets and Tania was muffled in a thick coat and gloves.
Gabe had tinsel around his browband and his harness
was covered in lots and lots of tiny Christmas bells.

"We've come to give you this," said Imogen, holding out a brightly wrapped present. "It's from us for you. Well, from Tania really."

"We really wanted to see you," said Tania. "And we thought it would be a fun thing to get Gabe to pull Imogen's sled." She smiled lovingly down at the little horse. "He's great at it and he hasn't had any trouble getting through the snow — he's as steady as anything."

Mandy grinned at her. "So he's not just a useless Miniature horse, then?"

Tania looked embarrassed. "I can't believe I was ever so stupid." She took the present from Imogen. "I brought you this to say thank you for making me realize how wonderful Gabe is."

Mandy took the present. It was a long thin cylinder. "Open it!" said Imogen. "Open it now."

She looked inquiringly at Tania, who nodded. "Yes, open it."

Mandy peeled off her gloves so she could take off the tape, and then finally got the paper off and took out a long, rolled-up tube. She unrolled it and gasped. It was an enormous poster of a spotted Miniature horse, just like Gabriel, with a thick, fluffy mane and tail and large, intelligent eyes. At the bottom of the poster were the words: *The Ambassador of Goodwill.*

"Merry Christmas!" said Tania.

"Do you like it?" Imogen demanded.

"I love it," Mandy said, grinning from ear to ear. She already knew where it was going to go — right above her bed!

"Aunt Sonia gave it to me for my birthday to go with Gabe," Tania explained. "It's a picture of Gabriel's father. But I want you to have it." She met Mandy's eyes. "As long as I've got Gabe, I know I can cope with anything."

"And you'll always have Gabe," Mandy said softly, looking at the little horse.

Tania nodded. "Animals are forever," she said. She put her arms around Gabe's neck and hugged him fiercely. "He's my horse and I am *never, ever* going to let him go."

Gabriel tossed his head, his dark eyes peeping at Mandy from under Tania's arm. That suits me just fine, he seemed to say.

Mandy smiled. "How's your dad, Tania?"

"Fine," Tania said with a happy smile. "He stayed for a little while last night but then went home because he was worried about the snow. I'm going to go and visit him. He's even said I can bring Gabe with me. He can stay in Star's old stable and paddock and I'll be able to see all my old friends."

Just then, the front door opened. "Tania! Imogen!" Dr.

Emily said. "Goodness, how did you get here through all this snow?"

"Gabe pulled me," Imogen said.

"Well, come in and have a hot drink and some pie," Dr. Emily said. "You must be freezing."

"What about Gabe?" Tania asked. "It'll be too cold for him to wait out here."

Mandy looked at her mom. "He could come into the kitchen, Mom," she said, her eyes pleading. "Just this once."

Dr. Emily hesitated and then gave in. "All right," she said with a smile. "I suppose it *is* Christmas, after all!"

They helped Imogen off the sled and, with lots of chattering and laughing, led Gabe inside. He stood by the kitchen table, looking rather surprised as Dr. Emily handed out mugs of hot chocolate and the pie. "Merry Christmas, everyone," she said.

Mandy got a plastic bowl and filled it with carrots. Gabe's tiny black ears pricked and he raised his head. She carried it over to him.

"Merry Christmas, Gabe!" she said.

Her eyes met Tania's and they both smiled.

Give someone you love a home!
Read about the animals of Animal Ark™